VICTOR X

T. H. RISS

World Castle Publishing, LLC
Pensacola, Florida
Copyright © 2024 T. H. Riss
Paperback ISBN: 9798891261501
eBook ISBN: 9798891261518
First Edition World Castle Publishing, LLC, March 11, 2024
http://www.worldcastlepublishing.com
Licensing Notes
Cover: Cover Designs by Karen
https://www.cover-designs-by-karen.com
Editor: Karen Fuller

To cousin Ermer. Thanks for the feedback and encouragement.

CHAPTER ONE

Earth, sometime in the future.

Life was complicated in the new world. Technological advancements had lifted many in society to new heights of wealth and power while at the same time leaving others behind in abject poverty. Modern machinery co-existed with relics from the past, and the gap between the haves and the have-nots only widened. As people became disenfranchised, they began to lose trust in government institutions and in the big corporations that seemed to hold most of the power. The dire warnings about the unchained growth of the military-industrial complex seemed prescient as the one thirsted for more power and the other for more money. Often lost in the obsession for progress was the sense of humanity upon which these institutions were founded, and at times, it seemed as if society had lost its way.

Victor X was employed as a telecommunication expert at BioTech Industries, where he had worked dutifully for the previous three years. He was of medium height with an athletic build, dark hair, and chiseled features. He wasn't married, and he didn't have a girlfriend, but he was socially active, often going out for drinks with his coworkers and playing doubles tennis with his neighbors Kelm, Margo, and Lacy. Victor did not recognize how exceptional he really was, not even on the day it happened, the day that would change the course of all the days that followed and elevate him in stature amongst the good peoples of this Earth.

Victor was a creature of habit, and every morning, he would rise, drink a cup of black coffee, and go cycling before leaving for work. He had a favorite route that took him through his own neighborhood and the one adjacent, a course that provided him with just the right amount of exercise intensity to satisfy thirty solid minutes of cardio. These rides were normally pleasant and uneventful until one morning in late March when something astonishing happened to disrupt his tranquility.

There were early signs that this would not

be an ordinary day. It began with a malfunctioning coffee maker that had failed to brew his favorite beverage and grew worse when he was forced to patch a flat tire on his bike before he could even begin his daily ride. But off he went, swooping through the parking lot and into the street, cranking up his pedaling rate until his legs were pumping like well-oiled pistons. The breeze was cool and dry that morning, and the sun appeared like a flaming meteor slowly climbing over the horizon, its red-orange glare reluctantly bending around the curvature of the Earth. He cruised briskly along the road until beginning a series of turns that would lead him through his course: up Courville Lane, right on Portsmouth, and then down the little dip that leads to Balfour Road. This is where he could really pick up the pace and lay down the rubber. He shifted up into a higher gear and raced down the street, feeling the cool air beat against his face and whistle through the vents in his helmet. He was fast approaching Nottingham, where he would have to begin downshifting to negotiate the tight turn. He gently squeezed the brake calipers as he decelerated into a lower gear and leaned into the curve, all the while checking for traffic, although it was typically sparse at that early hour. Nottingham provided him with the route's last long straightaway until it drifted into a lazy curve that would eventually lead him back toward his home. He shifted up through his gears and once again flew down the street at a rapid pace. But then, up ahead on the side of the road, just before the spot where the curve begins, he saw something that caught his eye. It appeared to be a large dog lying on its back, belly up, and rolling playfully in the tall grass. But as Victor drew nearer, things began to grow more sinister. The animal was tricolored: black and orange with a fluffy white belly. But then something else came into focus. "What's that?" thought Victor. "Looks red, like blood, maybe."

He squeezed the calipers and slowed down to a crawl as he approached the animal. He now realized it was not frolicking in the grass but writhing in agony, whimpering in a semi-conscious state of shock. He stopped the bike and laid it down on the curb as he carefully approached the dog. What he saw was unbelievable, unthinkable to him, but it appeared as if someone had started to skin the animal alive and had left it on the side of the road to die. Victor looked around for someone else, anyone at all, who might know something about this travesty or with whom he could at least share his sense of horror. But at that early hour of the morning, few people were out, and he was going to have to deal with it on his own. Victor crouched down and started to reach out to touch the animal but then reconsidered. What if it strikes back in anger, thinking he was the tormenter who committed this crime against nature, or perhaps it was rabid or diseased in some way? He looked closely at the wound and observed how the hide had been ripped away from the dog's pink flesh from just under its left front leg all the way down to its rear flank, the bright red blood staining the white underbelly of the animal in a cruel color contrast. It was a female, and she was clearly in a lot of pain. The nature of the wound indicated that this was no accident; this had been done intentionally with a sharp knife, and Victor knew he had to do something. But what? He couldn't exactly carry her on his bike, and he had left his mobile phone at home. He crawled on his hands and knees to where the dog's head lay and gently stroked her. "It's okay, girl, it's going to be alright. I'm going to get you some help."

Victor rose to his feet and assessed his options. He then sprinted up the sidewalk to the front porch of the nearest house to the accident scene, ringing the doorbell and rapping on the door vigorously until a woman finally answered.

"Hello, ma'am. I'm sorry to bother you, but we have an emergency. Do you know whose dog that is lying by the street?"

The woman glanced across her yard and spotted the dog in question. "Oh my! That looks bad." She looked back at Victor. "No, I have no idea who it belongs to. Never seen it before."

"Well, can you lend me a hand in some way? We've got to get that dog to a vet."

The woman sank back into her home and yelled for her husband to come to the door. He was a large, gruff-looking man still dressed in his robe and pajamas. "What can I do for you, bub?"

"We've got a situation with a severely injured dog down there in front of your house, and I don't have a car. Can you help me out?"

The man stepped onto the porch and glared down at the injured animal but then recoiled, shaking his head in dismay. "No, I'm sorry, but we can't help you," he mumbled as he retreated into his house.

Victor was shocked at receiving such a cold response. "Wait, what do you mean you can't help? She needs medical care, or she's going to die! We could at least drive her to the animal hospital."

The man angrily pulled the storm door closed. "I said we can't help you, and that's final! Call the cops or something. That dog's a goner anyway."

"Wait, I don't have a phone. Can you at least give me a towel or something to wrap her in until I can get her to a hospital?"

The man shook his head and disappeared, but the wife suddenly returned with an old, worn-out towel. "Here, mister, you can have this. Don't judge us too harshly. We're not bad people. It's just that we can't get involved with all the horrible stuff that goes on around here. We gotta protect ourselves, you know? And the cops, they won't show up even if we call. Here, take it." She handed Victor the towel and pushed the door closed.

"What the fuck!" he said to himself as he ran back down the sidewalk to the dog. He stood there momentarily frozen, unsure of what to do with the towel or why he had thought he needed it. But then he sprang into action, carefully rolling the animal on its side while placing one end of the towel on the grass, then gently rolling her down on top of the towel and pulling it around her body to the other side like a sort of tourniquet. She seemed to be in shock and was no longer writhing in pain. Having stabilized the dog, Victor jumped on his bike and pedaled home furiously, throwing caution to the wind and blowing through intersections without regard for his personal safety. Once he made it to the garage, he parked the bike and yanked off his helmet and gloves. He ran into the apartment to grab his phone, wallet, and key fob and then sprinted back down the stairs and jumped into his car, backing it out into the parking lot and then screeching his tires as he drove down the street.

It took only a few minutes to get back to the dog, and Victor pulled the car alongside the curb as near to the animal as possible. As he approached the dog, he noticed that her breathing had become quite shallow, but she was at least still alive. Victor crouched down and gently scooped up the animal, fearing that any pressure against her side would likely cause excruciating pain. But the dog surrendered willfully and fell limp into his arms, apparently too exhausted to cry out. He loaded her carefully into the rear of his car and closed down the hatch, sprinting back to the passenger door and jumping in. As he did so, he glanced up at the house he had visited and spotted the man and woman peeking out at him from behind their front window curtains. "Thanks for fucking nothing!" he yelled out the car window as it sped away from the curb.

"Nearest pet hospital to my location," he shouted into the car's navigation system.

The screen instantly lit up with directions. "Your destination is 5.6 miles away. You will arrive in ten minutes," responded the computer voice.

"Ten minutes? I hope she lives that long," said Victor. "Computer, ignore speed limits."

The autonomous vehicle selected the quickest route and deftly wove its way through the traffic as Victor tried his best to comfort the dog. The drive seemed as if it took forever, but the car finally pulled into the hospital parking lot and came to a stop just outside the front door. The lot was devoid of other vehicles, and there were no signs of activity inside the building. "What if the place isn't even open yet?" worried Victor. He jumped out of the car and ran to the front door, but just as he had feared, it was locked. He began pounding on the glass furiously and shouting for help. "Hello! Anybody in there? I've got a severely injured dog in my car, and I need some assistance."

A female doctor and a tech soon responded and unlocked the door.

"Come quickly. There's no time to lose,"

shouted Victor.

They all ran out to the car, and Victor raised the hatch, revealing his gruesome cargo. The doctor examined the dog, carefully peeling back the towel and inspecting the wound. "What the hell happened here? Is this your dog?" she asked.

"No, and I don't know what happened. I found her on the side of the road."

"Kyree, go get a stretcher board."

"Yes, doctor."

The doctor used her stethoscope to check the animal's heart and respiration. "She's barely alive. I don't know if we can save her, but we'll sure try." She gently stroked the dog's head. "You're gonna be okay, sweetie. That's a good girl. You just hang in there for me, okay?"

The tech returned with the stretcher board, and they carefully lifted the dog and placed her on it. Victor ran ahead and held the door as the medical team carried her into the hospital and then directly into the operating room, where they were joined by two more techs. The doctor began shouting commands, and the techs sprang into action, preparing the room for what was to come next.

"By the way, I'm Dr. Zhang," said the

woman as she turned her attention toward Victor.

"Hello, doctor. I'm Victor X," he said as they shook hands.

"Tell me again what you know about this dog."

"There's not much to tell. I was out cycling this morning when I found her writhing on the side of the road. I tried to enlist some help from a nearby house, but they declined and denied knowing anything about the dog. I saw how badly she was hurt and decided to bring her to the hospital. That's about all I know."

"Doctor," shouted one of the techs, "the operating room is ready."

"Thanks. I'll be right there." She turned back to Victor. "Mr. X, first, let me thank you for your act of kindness. Not everyone would have taken this action. Now, I would like for you to leave your name, address, and contact information at the front desk if you don't mind, and since this is not your dog, you're free to leave."

"Thanks, doc, but I'd like to hang around for a while if you don't mind. You know, to see how things turn out and all."

"Of course. You're welcome to wait if you'd like, but this could take quite some time. We do have some fresh brewed coffee over there in the corner. Now, please excuse me."

Dr. Zhang went into surgery, and Victor remained in the hospital lobby. The first thing he thought to do was to call BioTech and let them know he would be late for work.

"Hello, Marx, this is Victor. Listen, I had something personal pop up this morning, and I won't be in until later."

"You alright?"

"Yes, I'm okay. I'll tell you all about it later."

"You need the day off?"

"No, that won't be necessary."

"What about the simulation trials?"

"Tell Axle I'll take care of that this afternoon. It can wait."

"Yeah, okay. Talk to you later."

Victor ended the call and slipped the phone back into his pocket. He then walked over to the coffee pot, poured himself a cup of black coffee, and took a seat on the bench that lined the front window of the lobby. He had no idea how long the surgery would take, and he suddenly became concerned he might be waiting there all day. "Who knows how long it takes to put a dog back together," he thought. He sipped from his cup and looked up at the receptionist, who was peering intently at her computer screen.

"Excuse me, miss. Do you have any idea how long the doctor will be in surgery?"

She broke her gaze away from her computer. "No, I don't. But I'd be happy to check with one of the techs if you'd like."

"Sure, please do."

She rose from her desk and disappeared for a minute into the back room. Victor sipped from his coffee cup and stared out the window as another car pulled up and parked. The receptionist returned to her desk and called out to Victor. "Sir, they said probably another two hours or so, depending on the amount of damage they find."

"Okay, thanks for checking."

Just then, a woman walked into the lobby carrying a pet kennel. "Hello, my cat Pogo is here for her appointment," she announced joyfully to the receptionist.

"Okay, take a seat, Mrs. H, and we'll be right with you."

The lady sat down and placed the kennel on the bench right next to her. Victor could see that it contained a little white cat with gray dots on its side. The woman poked her finger through the cage and gently scratched the cat's ears while speaking in a soothing voice to keep the animal calm. The woman's doting kindness toward her pet was in stark contrast to the cruelty Victor had witnessed that morning. He finished his coffee and walked across the lobby to toss away the cup. He was feeling agitated, and he needed a way to kill some time to keep his mind off the dog. He walked outside for some fresh air and decided to call a friend.

"Hello, Kelm, this is Victor. What are you up to?"

"I'm working in my home office. Why? Are you at BioTech right now?"

"No, I had to call out. You're not going to believe what happened to me. I was cycling through my neighborhood this morning when I found an injured dog on the side of the road, so I went home, got my car, and brought her to the animal hospital."

"What a good Samaritan you are. What happened to the dog? Hit by a car?"

"No, Kelm, get this: Someone appears to have tried to skin the dog alive!"

"What? You're shitting me. Who would do a thing like that?"

"I know, that's what I've been wondering."

"What kind of dog is it?"

"Hell, I don't know. A big dog, calico in color, with a white belly. She's been in surgery now for about an hour. I'm hanging around to see if she makes it."

"Good for you. Not everyone would take such an interest in someone else's dog. Hey, did I tell you that Lacy got a new job?"

"No. I thought she liked her current job."

"She does, but she was offered a position as a systems manager at Ross-Lear Technologies."

"Ross-Lear? That's BioTech's main competitor."

"I know. I guess she'll be competing with you on and off the tennis court now!"

"Ha, we'll see about that. Anyway, tell her I wish her the best. I better let you get back to work. See you, Kelm."

Victor walked back into the lobby, which by then had filled with additional customers and their pet patients. "Any word on the dog?" he asked as he approached the receptionist's desk.

"No, I'm sorry, sir. Nothing yet."

"Do you have something for me to write on?"

She handed him a piece of paper and a pen.

"Here's my contact information. Have

someone call me immediately when the dog is out of surgery."

"Yes sir, will do."

CHAPTER TWO

BioTech Industries was one of the largest and most powerful companies in the world, making their fame and fortune as the leader in robotics and artificial intelligence (AI) technology. Victor X was employed there as a telecommunication specialist, where he helped design data and voice communication systems. He was sitting at his computer running data simulations when he received an important call.

"Mr. X, this is Kyree from the vet hospital. I just wanted to tell you that your dog made it successfully through surgery and is now resting under sedation in the recovery room."

"That's great news. How long was the surgery?"

"It took a good four hours to repair the

damage. She is an extremely sick but very lucky animal."

"I can only imagine what she has been through. Look, I'm at work right now, but I intend to leave early and stop by the hospital. Will I be able to see her?"

"You'll have to ask Dr. Zhang about that. I couldn't say for sure. That's usually not allowed, but I know this is a special circumstance."

"Alright. I'll see you later."

Victor leaned back in his chair and recalled some of the horrific images from earlier in the day, images that fueled his resolve to determine the identity and motivation of the dog's assailant. However, his contemplation was interrupted by the appearance of his supervisor.

"Hey Victor, Romy-3 wants to see you in the lab."

"Romy-3? What's that about?"

"Unknown. But she sounded adamant."

"Okay. Hey Axle, do you still need this data simulation report by tomorrow morning, or is there a little wiggle room? Something has come up, and I won't have as much time to spend on it today as I had originally planned."

"You mean because of what happened this

morning? Yeah, I can give you an extension. By the close of business, tomorrow will be fine."

"Thanks, Axle."

Victor rose from his chair and strolled down the hall to the telecom R&D lab, where he found Romy-3 consulting with another team member. He waited patiently for her to conclude her conversation.

"You wanted to see me Romy?"

"Yes, Victor. What is the status of that software robot project I assigned to you? I'm getting a lot of pressure from the top to submit our final proposal. It seems Ross-Lear is gunning for the same contract, and we can't afford to be cut off before we even get out of the blocks."

"It's the next thing on my list after I complete the AI simulation tests for Axle. I thought I had till next weekend to submit my work on the software robot?"

"Yeah, well, now that's changed. Can you have it to me in forty-eight hours? Thirty-six would be even better."

"Alright, I'll see what I can do."

Romy-3 walked toward Victor and glared at him. "Wrong answer, Victor. I don't need you to see what you can do; I need you to get it done."

Victor glared back at Romy-3, but he knew it was a no-win situation. "Alright, Romy. I'll get it done."

"Thank you, Victor," she said as she turned and walked away.

Victor returned to his desk and resumed his simulation tests with even more rigor than before. He still had a solid two hours to work on it before he would need to leave for the hospital, and thus far, the data was falling into accepted norms. The simulation was proceeding smoothly, and Victor was becoming even more optimistic about being able to finish the job quickly enough to also complete the project for Romy-3 within her new guidelines. He worked feverishly during the remaining time until he had reached a logical stopping point and then he shut down his computer and left the building for the parking lot. The advent of autonomous cars and their widespread usage greatly helped to control rush hour traffic but not eliminate it altogether. And drivers still had the option to override the controls and drive their own cars, a somewhat controversial feature allowed by the government at the behest of the automotive companies, even though it had the potential to disrupt traffic patterns and place others in danger. Nevertheless, Victor's car methodically wove its way through traffic until it reached the pet hospital with about twenty minutes to spare. He jumped out of the car and jogged into the building in time to catch Dr. Zhang, who was signing papers at the front desk.

"Hello, Dr. Zhang. I'm glad I caught you."

"Oh, hello, Mr. X. I didn't expect to see you again."

"Really? I told the tech earlier that I would stop by after work."

"Yes, but in these kinds of situations, where people bring in animals they find injured on the side of the road, we don't usually see them come back after our initial contact. They feel like they already did their good deed for the day, and they just move on with their lives. Are you sure she isn't your dog?"

"I told you she's not my dog. What happens to these stray animals?"

"Well, if we're lucky, we identify the owner, or we find an adoptive home for them."

"And if not?"

"We send them to a rescue shelter. On rare occasions, we have to euthanize them."

"You mean, you work hard to save them, and then you wind up putting them down anyway?"

"Yes, sometimes; isn't that crazy? But we're usually successful at adopting them out." Dr. Zhang continued with her paperwork. "Now, let's talk about the little friend you brought here earlier. She's had a rough go of it, that poor girl. But she made it successfully through the surgery, and she's resting comfortably under sedation right now. We're keeping a very close watch on her, as the next 24 hours will be critical in her recovery. But I can assure you that she's currently in no pain."

"That's good to know. How difficult was the surgery?"

"Oh, it was one of the most severe cases I have ever seen. We had to repair some subcutaneous damage and reattach her hide. It took a lot of staples to patch her up, I can tell you that. By the way, do you have a name for her? It seems strange to talk about her without a name."

"No, I...I haven't really thought about that. She's not my dog, after all."

"Well, if you don't mind, we've kind of given her a name because that's what we usually do in cases like this. One of the techs named her Angel because clearly, someone was looking out for her today."

"Angel...okay, I like that. We'll call her

Angel. Tell me, doc, do you often see cases like this? I mean, animals skinned alive?"

"Not often, thank God, but we do occasionally see them."

"What kind of a person would do such a thing?"

Dr. Zhang finished signing her paperwork and rose up from her chair. "A sick, sadistic person, someone who has no regard for the sanctity of life. It's hard to believe there are people like that out there."

"I know, it's hard to fathom. I wish I knew who Angel belonged to," said Victor.

"Oh, that reminds me," said the doctor, "we found a microchip imbedded under her skin."

Victor's eyes lit up with curiosity. "Really? So, we know who the owner is?"

"Not so fast. The information from the microchip doesn't necessarily prove ownership, and people often don't update the software associated with these chips. For example, the phone number we called was disconnected. But the information at least gives us a place to start."

"I suppose you've already reported this to the authorities, right?"

"Oh yes, I filed a report earlier today. But

you know, the agency is so short-staffed and overloaded with cases that there's no guarantee we will ever find out who did this."

"That sucks," said Victor as he paced around the lobby. "Listen, would it be possible for me to see Angel for a minute? I know you don't usually allow people back there, but this is kind of a special case."

Dr. Zhang smiled at Victor and nodded her head. "Yes, this is kind of a special case. Come on, I'll take you back there. But only for a minute. She needs her rest."

Victor followed Dr. Zhang through the doorway and into the recovery room, where he found Angel lying in bed, covered with a blanket and looking desperately pathetic. He walked nearer to the dog and leaned over to speak to her. "Hello, Angel. You've had a pretty rough day, haven't you?" He gently petted her on the head. "You're in good hands with Dr. Zhang, so you just rest up, and everything will be alright."

Angel opened her eyes and looked at Victor, and as she did, he and Dr. Zhang both noticed her tail twitch a couple of times.

"Did you see that, Victor! She knows who you are, and she's happy to see you."

"Yeah, how about that."

"Well, come on, Mr. X. That's enough excitement for her this evening."

Victor petted her one last time and saw Angel close her eyes. He then backed away from the table and followed the doctor through the door to the lobby. "Hey doc, do you think you could give me the information off the microchip? Maybe I could find out who Angel belongs to."

Dr. Zhang paused for a moment to think it over. "I suppose it would be alright, considering your noble intentions." She walked behind the receptionist's desk and jotted down the info on a piece of paper. "Here you go, for what it's worth. But don't forget, this info doesn't necessarily belong to the dog's true owner."

"I got it. Thanks doc. I'll be back tomorrow to check on Angel. Oh, and thanks for everything you've done."

Later that evening, while lying in bed, Victor began searching in his computer for the person identified by the microchip. It was someone named Adell K, a financial adviser who lived on the other side of town. Despite what Dr. Zhang had said, he wondered if this person could still be Angel's owner, and if so, how did the dog wind up on this side of town in such a horrible state? He closed the lid on his computer and turned off the light.

Victor reported early for work the next day so he could get a head start on finishing the project for Axle. He was running computer simulations and compiling data reports associated with AI development. The successful AI and software robotics programs offered by BioTech made them the industry leader, with Ross-Lear Technologies jealously nipping at their heels, and the reason why Romy-3 was pushing Victor to complete his work for her sooner than originally planned. But Victor had an even more compelling reason than business for completing these work projects: He now had Angel to think about. He completed the work for Axle and transferred all the results to him through the company's secure messaging system. Next, he turned to the software robotics assignment from Romy-3. He stayed late after work and completed the task under the thirty-six hours she had hoped for. Victor's work, as usual, was exemplary for these assignments, and he received praise from both Axle and Romy-3, who were now ahead of schedule for their individual projects. In return for his exemplary work, Victor requested and was granted leave time to address personal business, a thinly veiled excuse that would allow him to begin the search for Angel's owner.

The following morning, Victor wasted no time in beginning his quest. He jumped into the car and scanned directions into the navigation system, and the car's autonomous drive program took control as it guided the vehicle across town to the targeted address, a modest two-story home with tan colored bricks and red shutters. The house and yard seemed well manicured and, by extension, suggested to Victor that the resident might be a responsible pet owner. Victor exited his car and walked up the sidewalk to the front porch. He could hear the sound of music playing inside as he punched the security button. It took a minute, but the music subsided, and then someone unlatched the door, and it slowly opened to reveal a middle-aged woman, perhaps in her forties, with a pleasant smile and an equally pleasant demeanor.

"May I help you?"

"Are you, by chance, Adell K?"

"Yes, I am."

"My name is Victor X, and I was wondering if I might ask you a few questions about a dog I found."

"Are you with the police or SPCA?"

"Uh, no, ma'am. I'm just a concerned citizen; nobody really."

Sensing that Victor was no threat, Adell invited him inside. "Can I get you a drink or something?"

"No, thank you. I'll only be a minute. You see, I found this injured dog on the side of the road, and I took it to a veterinary hospital, where they located the ID microchip. It listed you as the owner, so I thought I'd check it out and see if it was still your dog."

"Oh my, I'm not sure. I have a little dog, but she's in the backyard right now." Adell rose up and peeked out the back window to reassure herself that her pet was indeed still there. "What does this dog look like?"

"She's a big dog, long hair, tricolored; orange, black, and white."

"That sounds like Callie! I had a dog like that a few years ago. Raised her from a puppy. The kids named her Callie, you know, like calico for the way she looked. Yes, I do remember getting her one of those microchips from the vet. You say she was injured?"

"Yes, quite severely, I'm afraid. You might not want to know the details."

"But she's still alive?"

"Yes, the last time I checked. Miss Adell, where did Callie go after she left your home?"

"Let's see, that was about five years ago. A neighbor had these Bernese puppies she was trying to adopt, and I went to her house and picked out Callie. She was so cute, with that little white squiggle on her forehead. And she seemed to be the most affectionate puppy in the litter. I raised her till she was about two, and then I donated her to a veteran who needed a comfort dog. Callie was the sweetest thing, very friendly and loving. The kind of dog that was perfect for a comfort pet."

"I see. Did you donate her to an organization or directly to an individual?"

"To an organization, you know, Pets for Vets or some such thing, I don't remember exactly. A gentleman came to my church one week and delivered a presentation that really spoke to me, and I thought that Callie would be a perfect candidate for such a service. I've always raised dogs and kept them as pets, and I thought, well, I could just get another one, you know, and let Callie be of service. I never did know with whom she was paired, but they assured me they would try hard to get her to the right person." Adell paused before continuing.

"Mister, I think you said your name was Victor? I'd like to know what happened to Callie."

Victor hesitated to tell the woman the truth but, under the circumstances, felt she deserved to know. "Adell, this is hard for me to tell you. You see, when I found Callie, it appeared as if someone had tried to skin her alive."

Adell sank back into her chair as if someone had just punched her. She put her hand up to her mouth and gasped for air. "Oh my God. Oh my God," she repeated in horror. "Why would someone do such an evil thing to such a sweet dog?"

"I'm sure I don't know, but I'm determined to find out."

Tears were now rolling down Adell's face. "They tried to skin her alive?"

"Yes, ma'am. But the important thing is she survived the surgery and has a good chance to recover."

"Not that a dog could ever recover from such trauma," whimpered Adell. "My poor sweet Callie…I would have never let her go if I knew this would happen."

Victor had no more to say, and he felt uncomfortable in the presence of the distressed woman. "Well, Miss Adell, I'm very sorry to have brought you such bad news, but I must be on my way. You're sure you don't remember the exact name of the service organization that received Callie?"

"No, I'm afraid not."

"Alright. Thank you for the information. I'll just follow the trail and see where it leads me." He rose to his feet and moved awkwardly toward the door.

"Thank you, Victor, for taking care of Callie in her time of need. God bless you for being such a kind soul."

"You're welcome, ma'am. Have a good day."

CHAPTER THREE

Victor called the Pets for Vets organization and told them what he was trying to do. They searched their records but said they could find nothing about a dog named Callie from five years earlier and could not locate a pet donor named Adell K. They suggested he check with other organizations that provided comfort pets to veterans, such as Healing Helpers. When he called Healing Helpers, they stated they did not give out such information over the phone, so he jumped in the car and drove to their local office. He met there with a woman named Trishton McCoy.

"Thanks for meeting with me, Ms. McCoy. My name is Victor X, and I'm sort of on a mission of mercy. You see, I found a severely injured dog on the side of the road the other day, and I'm trying to identify the owner. The doctor who treated her found a microchip implant and provided me with preliminary information. The dog seems to have originally belonged to a woman named Adell K, but she reports that she donated her dog to a charitable organization, one that provides comfort dogs to vets, but she was unsure of which agency. So, I've been calling around and trying to find someone who can help me."

"Okay, let's check the records and see what we come up with. When would this donation have occurred?"

"About five years ago."

Ms. McCoy began typing on her computer. "The donor's name again?"

"Adell K."

"And the dog's name at the time?"

"Callie."

"That name sounds familiar to me," the lady mumbled as she finished typing and scrolled through several screenshots. "Yes, here you go. I found her. Adell K donated a two-year-old Bernese Mountain dog named Callie. Does that sound right?"

"Yes!" Victor straightened up in his chair. "That sounds like the right dog. Can you tell me who she was given to?"

Ms. McCoy was reading the information contained on the dog's profile when a look of concern spread across her face. "I can tell you who she was given to, but I can't tell you who owns her now."

"What do you mean?"

"How did you say the dog was injured?"

"I didn't. But it was a most despicable thing. She was skinned alive."

"Oh my," gasped Ms. McCoy.

"But she has somehow survived the ordeal and is currently recovering after surgery. Do you know who she was given to?"

"Yes, she was assigned to a vet named Paxton Zinth. Sgt. Zinth was an amputee who lost his leg in combat while fighting in the steppes. Unfortunately, I remember this case very well…"

***

Five years earlier.

The woman knocked on the door of the man's apartment. He opened it and just stared at her.

"Hello. Are you Sgt. Zinth?"

"Yes. You must be the lady from Healing Helpers."

"I am. My name is Trishton McCoy, and this

is Callie," said the woman as she raised her hand and tugged gently on the leash attached to the dog by her side. "May we come in?"

"Yeah, sure. Please excuse the mess, but the maid hasn't arrived yet," he said sarcastically. As he backed away from the door, Ms. McCoy noticed that he was using a crutch.

"I see you're not wearing your prosthetic leg. I was under the impression over the phone that you had been fitted with one already."

"I do have a fake leg, but I took it off earlier. They don't tell you how uncomfortable those damn things are when they fit you for one. Why does it matter whether I wear one or not?"

"It makes no difference to me, but when we go to match a comfort dog with a recipient, it's important to understand just how mobile they are so we can find them the right dog."

"I'm mobile enough, I can assure you." He hopped across the room and cleared some newspapers off a chair for Ms. McCoy. "Here, take a seat."

She walked across the room with Callie following obediently at her side. "Well, like I said, this is Callie. She is two years old and a very sweet Bernese Mountain dog. She has completed her training in comfort school, which she passed with flying colors, I might add, and we think she would make a wonderful companion for you."

"Hmm, did you say her name was Callie?"

"Yes, short for calico, according to her donor."

"Well, that will have to change. I can't have no dog named Callie. Am I allowed to change the dog's name?"

"Well, yes, you are. Once a dog is assigned to you, it's your dog, and you can call her whatever you want, although we typically recommend you keep the name they're used to. It just makes things a lot easier. Would you like to pet her?"

"Sure," he said as he started to rise.

"No, Sgt. Zinth, just stay where you are, and I'll send her over to you." She detached the leash from the dog. "Callie, go over to Sgt. Zinth, and let him meet you."

Callie walked obediently over to Zinth, tongue sticking out the side of her mouth and tail wagging excitedly. She walked up to his chair and sat down beside him, putting on her friendliest and cutest face. He reached down slowly and let her smell his hand before petting her gently on the head. "She's a big dog, alright. I do like that. A man needs a big sturdy dog, not one of those little designer shits that celebrities carry around with them. Oh, excuse my language, miss."

"That's quite alright. Now, give her a simple command, like fetch the paper, for example."

Zinth stopped petting Callie and looked her in the eye. "Go get the newspaper, girl."

Callie walked over to where Zinth had tossed the paper and scooped it up with her mouth. She then spun around and brought it back to Zinth, sitting down next to him and waiting patiently for him to take it from her.

"Say, that's pretty good! What else can she do?"

"She can open and close doors if they're not locked, of course, she can fetch your mobile phone, help you cross the street, and bring your prosthetic to you. And with a little patience, you can teach her to fetch pretty much anything you want. She's a very quick learner."

Callie curled up and lay down at Zinth's feet.

"Aw, I think she's taken to you already, Sergeant."

Zinth reached down and petted her again. "Yeah, I think she has. Well, how does this work? I remember you saying there was some paperwork I needed to sign."

"Yes, I do have some papers for you to sign. As I explained on the phone, there will be a ninety-day trial period and if after that you still want her, we can finalize the adoption. Are you saying you want to give her a try?"

"Yeah, I'd like to give her a try. Let's do it."

Ms. McCoy zipped open the leather folder she was carrying and pulled out the temporary adoption papers for Zinth to read and sign. While he was doing that, she went down to her car and returned with a food bowl and some dog food.

"What about medical stuff for her?" asked Zinth.

"Callie is up to date on all of her immunizations. She is overall a healthy dog, but it's up to you to keep her that way. You shouldn't need another vet appointment for a year unless she gets sick or injured."

Zinth finished scribbling his name on all the papers. "Okay, it's a done deal. I guess I have a dog," he said as he petted Callie on the head. She, in turn, licked his hand and wagged her tail.

Ms. McCoy scooped up all her papers and placed them back in her folder. "Very well.

Congratulations, Sgt. Zinth. I think you will love having Callie as your companion. Don't hesitate to call me if you have any questions or problems to discuss. By the way, during this trial period, I'll be making some unannounced home visits just to make sure things are going smoothly. We are very particular about the pets we place and want to ensure this is a successful match for both you and her."

   With that being said, the woman departed, leaving the dog with Zinth so they could begin the bonding process. The first couple of days passed by uneventfully, and Zinth even took Callie out for a walk. However, he became annoyed every time someone complimented him on his beautiful dog and asked him for her name, for he viewed "Callie" as a sissy name for a man's dog. He resolved to rename her as soon as something more respectable came to mind. Next, he decided to teach her some new tricks. He taught her how to open the refrigerator and bring him a beer, a trick that took just a couple of days for her to master and a command that Zinth issued on a frequent basis as he was a heavy beer drinker. It was after she brought him a beer about a week later that he suddenly had a brainstorm over the name.

"I know what I can call you," he announced triumphantly, "I'll call you Barley! That's it, Barley after the main ingredient of my favorite beverage. Dog, you shall from now on be known as Barley. None of that Callie bullshit anymore," he told her as he patted her on the back.

Callie, who was now called Barley, was quick to accept her new moniker, so dedicated to pleasing her master was she. Things continued to progress smoothly, and Barley learned to fetch the newspaper from outside the apartment and how to open Zinth's car door for him. Although he was not blind, Zinth experimented with closing his eyes briefly to see if the dog could successfully lead him around, which he quickly discovered she was more than capable of doing as long as he held her leash tightly by his side. It became one of his favorite pranks to pull on friends and strangers alike, to feign blindness and garner sympathy from people, only to embarrass them when he finally let on that he was able sighted. Barley even seemed to enjoy the ruse, as she would bark and wag her tail excitedly as her owner howled with laughter after revealing the truth. Zinth and Barley seemed to be getting along well, and they passed inspection whenever Ms. McCoy would make one of those unannounced visits.

But Zinth also had his dark side. He had been diagnosed with PTSD from his combat days, which caused him to have bouts of depression. And he had anger management issues associated with the loss of his leg. As a result of these conditions, he would often self-medicate, usually by consuming large quantities of beer, although he was not opposed to using illicit drugs on occasion as well. He often complained to whoever was willing to listen that the VA was useless for helping him with his medical needs. When he was depressed or wakened from sleep with night sweats, he'd call for Barley, who would comfort him by jumping into bed and cuddling until either the mood would pass or Zinth fell back asleep. But when he was angry, which happened often when he drank too much, he would take it out on her by calling her a "dumb bitch" or hurling his prosthesis at her, or poking at her with his crutch. Barley seemed to understand that he didn't mean it, and during these times, she would stay out of his way by curling up in the corner until he needed her again.

Zinth would, on occasion, attend veteran support group meetings, although he questioned the value of "whining about my troubles in front of a whole group of whiners." However, comfort dogs were welcomed at these meetings, and shortly after adopting her, Zinth took Barley with him to a session. He proudly introduced her to the others at the meeting and bragged about her sturdy build and exceptional intelligence. It seemed as if he attended the meeting more to just show off his dog than to seek help managing his demons.

"Sgt. Zinth, we haven't heard from you lately," said the group leader on one occasion. "And we've never heard the story about how you lost your leg. Are you willing to share with us today?"

Zinth squirmed uncomfortably in his chair before responding, but the presence of Barley seemed to give him the will to proceed. "It's not that I'm afraid to talk about what happened. I just don't think most people really give a damn. But I suppose that's different here. As y'all know, we've been fighting the Chinese now for almost five years. Ironically, despite our technological advancements, the threat of a nuclear confrontation limits our engagements to the use of more traditional weaponry, and much of the fighting has taken place on the steppes. I was riding in an APC on a scouting patrol along the eastern ridge where a lot of movement had been reported over the previous

24 hours."

"Excuse me. The others probably know, but what is an APC?" asked the group leader.

"It's an airborne patrol craft designed to carry up to five troops. We were hovering low to the ground to avoid detection when we were suddenly struck by a Chinese RPG. We could normally withstand a hit like that, but this one had armor-piercing capability. The damn thing blew right through the bottom of the APC, and as luck would have it, I was sitting in just the right spot to take a direct hit. The fucking thing blew off my leg, and we hit the ground like a stone. The Chinese were suddenly swarming all over us like ants on an anthill, and a firefight ensued. One of my buddies quickly tied a tourniquet around my stump, and I fired my weapon until I ran out of ammo. His quick thinking saved my life because there was no time for medical attention. Somehow, we repelled the attack and called in air rescue, and I had my one-way ticket back home. But I wish I was still back there with my buddies. I feel useless over here."

Although the details may have differed, the story Zinth told was one the group had often heard from others. The harsh reality of war had not only torn their bodies but also ripped away at their psyche. One Sunday afternoon, Zinth took Barley out for a walk, and it wasn't long before they wound up at the corner bar. Barley was familiar to the bar owner and allowed inside because of her status as a comfort animal. She lay on the floor at Zinth's feet while he slugged down several schooners of beer. He would occasionally toss her a peanut but otherwise basically ignored her. The more Zinth drank, the louder and more belligerent he got, and soon, he was in a heated argument with a Navy vet over whose military service was more honorable.

"The fighting on the steppes was brutal," complained Zinth. "It was often hand to hand combat, man to man...none of this bullshit where you lob missiles from twenty miles offshore. You ain't ever killed a man unless you looked him in the eye and felt his breath on your face while sticking a knife in his chest."

The Navy vet slammed his beer glass down on the table. "That's a bunch of grunt bullshit! How come the U.S. Navy has had to bail you guys out on more than one occasion if you grunts are such badasses. I'm sick of hearing you cry about how tough it was on the steppes. Fuck the steppes and fuck you, you fucking loser."

Zinth rotated on his barstool and tried to

launch a punch at the Navy vet, but before he could swing, the man landed his own punch on the side of the sergeant's face, knocking him senseless to the ground. "Get up, you fucking loser, and I'll hit you again!"

But Barley would have none of that. She jumped into action, not attacking the man but taking a protective stance in front of Zinth, growling and baring her teeth.

"That's it, hide behind your bitch, grunt."

Zinth was furious. He pulled himself up to his feet, grabbed Barley by the collar, dragged her out of the bar, and threw her into the street. He barged back through the door to address his nemesis. "I don't need no fucking bitch dog fighting my battles. Come here, you cockeyed son of a bitch, and I'll kick your ass!"

The man ran at Zinth and knocked him out with one punch before the bartender could intervene. Within minutes, the authorities were at the bar, and Zinth was receiving medical attention. Neither man wanted to press charges, and after hearing their story, the cops released them both on their own recognizance. The bartender called a cab for Zinth, who seemed to forget all about Barley.

"Hey, Zinth," yelled the bartender, "don't

forget your dog."

"Fuck her. She can find her own way home," he said as he slammed the door shut on her.

Barley did find her way home, and later that evening, she scratched at the door until Zinth finally got up and let her in. He passed out on the bed, and she cuddled next to him like she often did.

Although the agency would frequently ask the neighbors for feedback, no one was willing to share any damning information about Zinth, perhaps out of sympathy for his condition and appreciation for his service. So, despite the rough times, Zinth and Barley made it through the ninety-day trial period, and the adoption was finalized. That meant Ms. McCoy would no longer be dropping by for unannounced visits, and the sergeant could quit trying to be on his best behavior. The neighbors would often hear Zinth shouting at his dog and throwing things in his apartment in a drunken rage, but then they would see him playing with her in the yard or proudly introducing her to strangers who marveled at all the tricks she could perform on command. This dysfunctional relationship between the big, friendly dog and the mean-spirited man lasted for almost three years, and the neighbors wondered why Barley didn't just run away from him when she had the chance. But she never did, and she remained loyal to Zinth until the end.

***

"So, whatever became of Sgt. Paxton Zinth?" asked Victor X.

"As you can imagine, the story has a tragic ending," said Ms. McCoy. "I've gleaned all this information from interviewing neighbors and researching police records. It seems that Zinth became addicted to a powerful prescription opioid, and when he couldn't get enough of the stuff through his doctors, he would buy it on the streets. On one of those occasions, he took Barley with him, and during the exchange, something went wrong. Zinth may have argued over the price, or he may have tried to knock off the dealer for his supply, but it's clear a fight ensued. Bystanders reported that Zinth became incensed when one of the gang members pistol-whipped his dog when she tried to intervene. At any rate, Zinth was shot but able to stumble away a short distance. He was found dead in an alley near his apartment several hours later, but the dog was never seen again. That's the last I heard about Barley or Callie, as I knew her until you contacted me."

"Are you sure about the timeline? You said

that Callie was with Zinth for about three years, but the adoption took place five years ago. So, where has she been in the meantime?"

"I have no idea, Mr. X. That's all the information I've been able to gather about Callie."

Victor rose from his chair and extended his hand to Ms. McCoy.

"Thank you very much for your time and all the information, Ms. McCoy. You've been a great help to me. I'll be on my way now."

"What are you going to do? How are you going to find Callie's owner?"

"I don't know. It seems as if I've hit a dead end. But I'm not giving up."

CHAPTER FOUR

Victor was working at his desk when his unit leader, Axle, ordered him to the clinic. The monthly visit to the company clinic was required for all team members to ensure unit productivity and was perceived by Victor as a generous perk of his employment. He rode the elevator down to the clinic and dutifully reported to the doctor, who had Victor lie down as he clipped a monitor to his finger and placed electrodes on his torso and head. He instructed Victor to remain still for several minutes while the diagnostics were running, and soon enough, he was back at work at his desk. If it weren't for the fact that everyone in his unit made these monthly visits, Victor would wonder if there wasn't something wrong with him that required such rigorous monitoring. However, no one else complained about these minor disruptions to their workday, so Victor took them in stride.

Victor had become so proficient at his job that he was outperforming everyone else in his unit and had temporarily run out of project assignments. For that reason, and for others that he was unaware of, he was reassigned to Romy-3 until further notice. She had made this request following Victor's exemplary performance on the software robotic assignment, arguing that Victor's unique approach to solving problems would enhance the productivity of the research and development projects coming out of her lab. Victor liked working for Axle, whose management style he perceived as directive but fair and with whom he rarely had a disagreement. However, in his brief encounters with Romy-3, Victor had found her to be confrontational and domineering, although quite intelligent. It was no secret that she was one of BioTech CEO Kyan Quantum's favorite employees, and it was a well-known fact that her lab generated most of the company's profits, so Victor perceived the reassignment as a leg up on the corporate ladder.

On the day that Victor reported to the R&D lab for the first time, Romy-3 was out of the office on assignment, so an engineer named Jericho showed him around. "Good to have you aboard, Victor. I've heard a lot of good things about you from Romy."

"Thanks. I'm pleased to be reassigned to the R&D lab. Tell me, besides software robotics, what other stuff do you guys have on your plate?"

"I must say software robotics has taken up most of our time lately since we're being seriously challenged by Ross-Lear for our government contract. And, of course, we're always working on ways to perfect the humanoid design features. But you know all about that from your work with Axle."

"Yes, I've put in a lot of hours running simulations and crunching data for him."

"What's it like over there, working with Axle, I mean?"

"It's good. We have a real close team. And he gives us a lot of room to be creative."

"That's what I hear. I think you'll find it a little different working under Romy-3. She's a no-nonsense type of leader, real hands-on, if you know what I mean. But I tell you, I've never worked for a more intelligent manager than her. She has a feel for robotics like no one I've ever met, although based on what she tells me, you're in the same category."

"What do you mean?"

"Just that it takes a certain kind of mind, a gift really, to envision the potential in robotics. Hey, I meant it as a compliment, son," laughed Jericho.

Victor spent the rest of the afternoon reading through rough drafts of future design projects while trying to envision what he might bring to the table. He wasn't an engineer like Jericho, but obviously, Romy-3 cherished his telecommunication skills, or she wouldn't have gone after him so hard. In the meantime, he was looking forward to paying a visit to the animal hospital to check on Angel's progress. He was anxious to bring Dr. Zhang up to date on what he had learned about Angel's history while at the same time hoping that she might have an idea about how to pick up the owner's trail, which had suddenly grown cold. Victor was in the process of shutting down for the day when Axle popped into the lab to wish him well. "Hey Victor, how was your first day in the R&D division?"

"Hi, Axle. Pretty uneventful. Romy-3 was out of the office today, so Jericho did the orientation. I'm looking forward to meeting with her, but I already miss you guys."

"Ah, you'll fit in nicely over here. They need your expertise. But I stopped by for another reason.

Your ex-teammates and I would like to meet you for drinks after work. How about it?"

"Yeah, sure, that sounds great. I want to first stop off at the animal hospital to see Angel, but I can meet you guys later. At the usual place?"

"Yeah, the usual place. We'll hold a seat for you. I hope that Angel is feeling better. See you later."

After leaving work, Victor made the drive across town to the vet hospital, where he hoped to see improvement in Angel's condition. He checked in at the receptionist's desk, but by then, everyone knew who he was and why he was there. He waited in the lobby until one of the techs could escort him to the recovery room.

"Good evening, Mr. X. I'll take you back to see Angel now." said the tech named Kyree. She led Victor to the recovery room, and as soon as Angel heard his voice, she began wagging her tail. "Look who's come to visit you, Angel. Your friend Victor is here."

Victor walked nearer to the table and Angel lifted her head to better see him. He reached out and gently stroked her fur while she whimpered softly.

"Her demeanor always improves the minute

you arrive, Mr. X. I think you have a real friend for life."

Just then, Dr. Zhang entered the recovery room. "Hello, Mr. X. Our patient is recovering quite nicely. I think we can say that she is finally out of the woods, although she still has a lot of healing to do."

"That's good news. How long before the staples can be removed?"

"Oh, it'll still be a few more days before we can consider that. But I'm very happy with her progress. Any luck with finding the owner?"

"Yeah, I've made some headway but temporarily hit a dead end. I told you about Adell K, and now I know the story about the vet who received Angel through Healing Helpers. His name was Paxton Zinth, an amputee who was dealing with PTSD. According to the neighbors, he also had some anger management issues and took it out on the dog on many occasions. Angel must have had a pretty rough time with him. She was with Sgt. Zinth for about three years until he was killed in a bad drug deal, and then the trail goes cold. I have no idea where she's been the past two years. Do you have any suggestions about how to proceed?"

Angel began licking Victor's hand as he had

stopped petting her. "Am I ignoring you, Angel? Is that what you're trying to tell me?" he said as he began petting her again.

"No, I'm afraid I don't have anything helpful to suggest," said Dr. Zhang. "You've done a great job learning as much as you have so far. Maybe that's all we're going to get."

"I hope not. I won't be satisfied until I can trace it all the way back to the person who did this. By the way, any word from the authorities regarding their investigation?"

"No. Like I told you before, they are overwhelmed. My experience tells me that Angel is a low priority since she has already been rescued and is receiving medical care. They're likely focusing on reports of animals still in harm's way. The simple fact is society doesn't care enough to provide the proper resources for animal protection agencies."

"What if I come up with the name of the person who did this?"

"Then I think they would be very interested in prosecution."

Victor continued petting Angel for another minute, and then he leaned over and kissed her on the head. "I'm sorry, but it's time for me to go,

Angel. You be a good girl and get well soon."

Victor and Dr. Zhang left Angel's side and walked toward the lobby.

"Mr. X, this is a delicate subject, but Angel's medical bills are piling up, and although you are technically not responsible for her…"

"Dr. Zhang, you need not go any farther. I'll be happy to pay her medical bills."

"Oh my, that is very generous of you, but I wasn't going to suggest that. We do a lot of charitable work here at the hospital, but as you can imagine, it gets very expensive. Perhaps you could make a small donation to the hospital in Angel's name; that would suffice."

"Of course. I'll transfer some funds to your hospital later tonight. And if you need anything else for Angel, consider it done."

"Thank you, Mr. X. Angel has found a true patron in you."

Victor exited the hospital and drove back across town to the bar where he was to meet his coworkers. They were all there: Axle, Marx, Claiborne, Marcus G, and Sizemore. They all waved at Victor when he entered through the doorway, and he took a seat amongst his friends. There were already two pitchers of beer on the table, so Victor poured himself a glass.

"Well, how did it go? How was Angel tonight?" asked Axle.

"She's doing lots better. According to Dr. Zhang, she's out of immediate danger but still has a lot of healing to do."

"I can imagine that. I was just telling the others the story about how you found her."

"Victor," asked Marcus G, "did someone really try to skin that dog alive?"

"Yes, unfortunately, that's true."

"I swear to God, if I ever caught someone doing a thing like that, I'd take great pleasure in kicking their ass!" added Sizemore.

"I know what you mean. I'm doing my best to try and figure out who did it, but the dog has changed owners multiple times, and I'm not even sure who she belongs to," replied Victor.

"What kind of a dog is she?" asked Claiborne.

"She's a Bernese Mountain dog, a beautiful animal, tricolored like a calico cat. Friendly as hell and loyal, too, from what I've been able to learn. It's a shame to think something like this would happen to such a noble creature."

Victor took a swig from his beer glass as a waitress approached the table. "Excuse me, gentlemen, but I couldn't help but overhear your conversation. Did you say you're looking for the owner of a big fluffy mountain dog that has a calico coloring?"

Everyone looked at Victor. "Yes, that's true," he answered. "Why, do you have a dog like that?"

"Well, I used to, but I don't anymore." The woman began writing on a piece of paper. "I can't talk right now, but here's my name and contact information. Call me later," she said as she handed him the note and walked away.

"Whoa, look at Victor, making it with the ladies!" hooted Marx.

"It's nothing like that, I'm sure," said Victor sheepishly. "Besides, she's not even my type."

"Oh yeah? And what type is that?" laughed Axle. "How about Romy-3? Is she your type?"

The others all groaned.

"Yeah, I hear she's a real tigress, if you know what I mean," added Marcus G.

"I don't know Romy-3 enough to judge anything about her personal life. I only know she's intelligent and the foremost expert on AI at BioTech," said Victor.

"You mean other than Quantum. He's the real brain behind the AI program. That's how BioTech pushed ahead of Ross-Lear for the government contracts," explained Axle.

"Well, as far as Romy-3 and your transfer to her division is concerned, better you than me," added Sizemore laughingly.

"I'll drink to that. Here's to Victor and his new gig with R&D," toasted Marcus G.

"Hear, hear!" they all said as they lifted a glass in honor of Victor.

The next morning, Victor met with Romy-3, who had returned from her assignment outside the office. She picked up the employee orientation where Jericho had left off. "I hope you're excited about being transferred to my division. I know I'm excited to have you here."

"I am pleased to be given the opportunity to expand my horizons, and I'll do my best to be an asset for R&D," he replied.

"Good answer. And I'm sure that you will be an asset. You know, Dr. Quantum is relying on us to drive the AI program to the next level, and to that end, your telecommunication skills will be of great value. I want to show you something that not many people, even Dr. Quantum, know about. Look here." Romy-3 rotated her computer screen toward Victor and punched a key. Data began to flow across the screen at a rapid pace, but he had no trouble keeping up with the coding.

"What is this? I've never seen anything quite like it. This is a whole new language capable of communicating complex data at twice the speed as the simulations I was running for Axle."

"Exactly. This is where AI is headed, and you will be at the tip of the spear. I don't think I need to tell you how important this is to the U.S. government."

Victor continued staring at the screen until Romy shut the program down and spun the monitor away from him. "You'll be helping me perfect this language for the next several weeks or months, or however long it takes. But keep in mind, around here, time is always of the essence. And I don't suffer missed deadlines very well."

"Understood. I won't let you down."

"I know you won't, Victor, or I wouldn't have asked for you."

CHAPTER FIVE

Victor drove up and parked his car in front of Building C in the apartment complex on the east side of town, a section of the city known for its low-income housing. Each building in the complex contained twenty housing units evenly divided on two floors. The architecture was utilitarian, and only a modicum of effort was put into the landscaping surrounding the property. He strolled around the corner and up the stairs to unit 224-C and rang the doorbell. As the door slowly opened, Victor recognized the face of the waitress from the bar two nights earlier.

"Hello. I'm Victor X, the man you spoke to at the bar the other night."

"Hello, Victor, I'm Larene Langston. Come on in."

Victor stepped inside the tiny apartment and noted the colorfully painted walls and matching furniture. "I love the way you've decorated your apartment."

"Oh gosh, thank you. It's not much; this is all second-hand stuff, but I'm grateful for everything I have. I try hard to make it as nice as possible for the kids' sake. Thanks for noticing. Please have a seat."

Victor sat down on a chair near the window overlooking the parking lot.

"After giving you my name at the bar, I wasn't sure if you would call me, but I'm glad that you did," said Larene.

"Really? Why wouldn't I call you?"

"Oh, I don't know. It felt a little forward of me, and I heard your friends make fun of you as I walked away."

"You should ignore that. Just friendly banter. They meant no harm."

There was an awkward pause.

"Okay," she said clumsily, "where do we start?"

"Well, how about we make sure we're talking about the same dog. She's a big female Bernese Mountain dog, about ninety pounds, with a long coat with black, rust, and white colors. About seven years old, and she has a distinctive white squiggly line between her eyes that extends to the top of her head."

"Yes, that's her! That's the same dog I had."

"Okay, when did you get her, and how long did you have her?"

"Well, it was about two years ago when we first got Rusty — that's what the kids named her — but she just showed up at the house one day…"

***

Two years earlier.

It was nearly the end of summer vacation, and the children were playing in the front yard. Toi, at ten years the oldest child, was pushing Markie and Cadence in the wagon when she just appeared out of nowhere; she being a big black dog with a funny white mark on her face. She walked right up to the children and sat down as if she belonged there.

"Hey, who are you?" squealed Toi as she petted the dog's long black coat. "You're a pretty girl, except you need a bath!"

Markie and Cadence crawled out of the wagon and knelt alongside the dog, each reaching out and petting her gently.

"Ooh, look, blood," said Cadence as he

pointed to the dried red stain on the dog's head.

"I wonder whose dog she is?" asked Markie, the oldest boy.

"I don't know, but she has a collar, so she belongs to somebody," observed Toi.

"I think she looks thirsty," said Cadence.

"You're right. She sure does look thirsty. I'll go get her some water." Toi ran into the house and found a small pan suitable to use as a water bowl.

While Toi was at the sink filling the pan, her mother came into the kitchen. "What are you doing, Toi?"

"I'm getting some water for the dog."

"What dog?"

"The one in the front yard."

The woman looked out the window and saw the dog with her two children. "Whose dog is that?"

"I don't know, Mom. She just showed up," said Toi curtly as she left the kitchen with the pan of water. Her mom held the door open for Toi as she stepped carefully down the stairs and onto the cement walkway that led up to the house. She continued her journey to the front lawn and carefully placed the pan down before the dog.

"I told you she was thirsty," laughed Cadence as the dog vigorously lapped the water from the pan.

"Have you kids ever seen this dog before?" asked the mother.

"No, Momma, she just appeared," answered Markie.

"Look, she has a collar," said Toi.

The woman bent down next to the dog and gently grabbed hold of the collar to inspect it. "Yes, she does. She has a rabies tag but no other identification. Clearly, she belongs to somebody," said the mother as she continued inspecting the dog. "Somebody who doesn't take good care of their dog. Looks like the cut on her head has healed, but her coat is dirty and a tangled mess, and I bet she hasn't had a good meal lately either."

"Can we keep her, Momma? Please, please, please," squealed Markie.

"No, we can't keep her, Markie. I just said I think she belongs to somebody. You can't just take somebody's dog."

"But maybe she's lost or abandoned, or maybe she just ran away from home," said Toi.

"Maybe, but she probably lives around here somewhere. She sure is a friendly thing," said the woman as she petted the dog. "Dogs are pretty good at finding their way back home, so we should just leave her alone. Come on in the house, kids. It's time for lunch."

The mom and her three children said goodbye to the dog and retreated to the house for lunch. They forgot about the dog for the next hour, but when the children ran back outside to play, they found her sleeping peacefully on their porch.

"Look, Toi, she's still here!" said Cadence excitedly.

"Oh my gosh. You're supposed to go home," ordered Toi. But the dog remained curled up on the porch with clearly no intention of leaving. She remained there for the rest of the afternoon while the children played. She was still there when their father returned home from work just in time for dinner.

"Daddy, Daddy, look what we found," screamed Cadence as he ran to his father's arms. "A dog!"

The father looked up at the front porch and noticed the dog curled up in a ball. "Well, I'll be... Whose dog is that?"

"We don't know," said Toi, "but she doesn't seem to want to leave."

The dad walked over and petted the dog, who immediately began wagging her tail and looking for sympathy. "If you cleaned her up, I bet she'd make a pretty nice pet."

"Jax, kids, time for dinner," yelled Larene from the house.

"Come on, kids, Mom's calling us."

Jax scooped up Cadence into his arms and herded the other kids into the house for dinner. Larene tried to ask Jax about his workday, but the children could not stop talking about the stray dog on the front porch.

"Daddy, can we keep the dog?" asked Toi.

"Your mother and I will have to talk about it. But Toi, I'm sure she's already told you that we have an obligation to try and find the owner."

"I know, but if we can't find the owner, can we keep her?"

"We'll see. Now, eat your dinner and quit pressing me about that dog."

After dinner was finished and the dishes were cleared, Larene peeked outside at the front porch. The dog was still there, so she made a plate of food with leftovers and took it out to her. She set the plate down and stood back as the dog eagerly attacked the food, glancing back at the woman occasionally as if to express her gratitude. Jax had been looking for Larene when he found her out on the porch with the dog. "Aren't you the soft touch," he said to her.

"I know, I can't help it, Jax. She's such a pitiful thing. It makes me wonder where she's been and what she's been through."

"You do agree that we've got to at least try to find the owner."

"Of course. She has a rabies tag, so I'll make a few phone calls tomorrow and see if I can't identify the owner. In the meantime, I'll start asking around the neighborhood as well. Will you post something on social media?"

"Sure, I'll take care of that tonight."

"Jax, if things work out, you don't mind if we keep her, do you? We've talked about getting the kids a dog in the past, and maybe it's fate that she showed up on our doorstep."

"No, I don't mind. She seems friendly enough. And as big as she is, she might actually make a good nanny pet for the children. Let's just see how it plays out."

The dog had finished eating her food and had walked over to where Larene was kneeling. She began nuzzling her arm and licking her hand, demanding to be petted.

"Aw, look at her, Jax. What a sweet girl. But

oh boy, do you need a bath!"

Over the next several days, Jax and Larene tried their best to identify the dog's owner. Through the rabies tag, they found out about Paxton Zinth, but further research revealed he was deceased. Whether or not the dog had been passed on to someone else, they could never determine, and during that time, they had all become attached to the dog. Although the tag identified the dog's name as Barley, the children had already begun calling her Rusty after the orange color that ran through her coat. They discovered quickly how smart the dog was, and they were easily able to train her to obey commands and perform tricks, some of which she clearly already understood, like opening doors and fetching things. Rusty bonded with the children instantly and became very protective of them, enhancing Larene's sense of security. She observed Rusty standing guard over the children while they played in the front yard, positioning herself on the edge of the lawn where she could ward off strangers. Someone had obviously spent a lot of time training that dog, and she had learned her lessons well.

Over the ensuing months, everyone in the neighborhood got to know Rusty, and they took great joy in watching her interact with the children. When the family would take her for walks, strangers would often approach and ask permission to pet the giant mountain dog. Rusty would sit there obediently and allow people to fawn over her, and she became an ambassador of sorts for all those in the neighborhood. Toi even taught Rusty to do favors for the elderly lady next door, like pulling her little grocery cart home from the corner store, and Cadence and his friends would take turns sitting on her back and riding her around the yard as if she were a small pony. After surviving her tumultuous existence with Sgt. Zinth, Rusty had come home to a place where she was loved unconditionally and never abused. The Langstons were the picture-perfect little family, with two loving parents, three healthy children, and a big fluffy dog that everyone loved. After struggling for years at the bottom of the economic strata, the family was finally on their way up. Until it all came crashing down that fateful day when the police car pulled up in front of the house. The officer walked slowly up the sidewalk and knocked on the front door.

"Hello, Mrs. Langston?"

"Yes, that's me."

"You have a husband named Jax?"

"Yes. Is there something wrong?"

"I'm afraid so, ma'am. You see, your husband has been in a terrible car accident."

"A car accident? But he has an autonomous car."

"I know, but something went wrong."

"Oh my God!" she exclaimed while wiping her hands on her apron. "Wait here while I put on my shoes and grab a sweater. I'll need you to drive me to the hospital. We only have the one car."

"No, wait, Mrs. Langston. He's not at the hospital."

Larene stopped and stared at the officer, and the look on his face was worth a thousand horrible words. Tears began to well up in her eyes, and she shook her head in disbelief. "No, no," she just kept repeating. "You're telling me he's gone, aren't you?"

"Yes, ma'am. I'm sorry, but there was a fire, and…I'll need you to identify his body at the morgue."

Larene was frozen and unable to move until Toi came to the door and saw her mother crying. "What's the matter, Momma?"

Larene knelt down next to Toi and squeezed her tight. "Something has happened to Daddy, and

I have to go see about it."

"What's happened to Daddy?" asked Toi as she began to cry.

"I'll tell you later," said Larene as she gently separated from Toi. "Listen, Toi, I need you to be my big girl. I need you and Rusty to watch after Markie and Cadence until I get back. I won't be long. Can you do that for me?"

"Yes, Momma," responded Toi as big tears rolled down her cheeks.

Larene stood back up and faced the officer. "I'll be right with you."

The premature death of Jax Langston was a catastrophic blow to the little family. Larene had come from a broken home and was one of millions of citizens who were left behind without a skillset to match the ever-spiraling demands placed on the modern workforce by technological advances. Jax, on the other hand, had the education and the expertise to advance high enough in his company to finally make a respectable living for his wife and kids. But now, without him in the picture, Larene was faced with an uncertain future. She spoke to an attorney about compensation, and there was a possibility that the car manufacturer could be held liable for the accident, but it would be an ongoing battle that would have to weave its way through the court system. Jax's employer, fortunately, covered the funeral expenses, but there were groceries, utility bills, a new car payment, and a mortgage to pay, and Larene had limited earning potential. She was eventually able to land a job as a waitress, but it wasn't enough to sustain their current standard of living. After much consideration, through many sleepless nights, she decided they were going to have to leave their home and move into an apartment.

***

"Larene, I'm so sorry about your husband," offered Victor.

   "Thank you. I still cry about it sometimes. Jax was a good man, hard to find nowadays. Anyway, as I was saying, I couldn't afford to stay in the house any longer. We were barely making it on Jax's salary as it was. We received some donations and money from his life insurance policy, but he had no pension or anything like that. I don't have much of an education, so the best I could do was wait tables. Don't get me wrong, waiting tables is an honorable trade, and sometimes I even make pretty good money, but not like what Jax was earning. So, I sold most of our stuff and started looking for a low-income apartment to move into."

"What did the children think about that?"

"Oh, they were devastated. They didn't want to leave their house or their neighborhood, but we had no choice. The bills were piling up, and I was afraid we'd go bankrupt, and I might lose the kids if I didn't do something. I finally found this little two-bedroom apartment, and I took it. I figured the boys could share one bedroom, and Toi could have the other. I would just sleep on the couch for the time being, but you know what? Toi insisted I take the other bedroom, and she would sleep on the couch. She's such a sweet girl."

"What about Rusty?"

"I'm getting to that part. There is a serious lack of affordable housing in this city, and try as I may, I couldn't find a place I could afford that would accept dogs, and even if I did, I couldn't afford the extra deposit required for pets. Believe me, I tried hard. I loved that dog as much as the kids...well, maybe not as much as them because you know how kids are with dogs, but I loved Rusty. I considered just sneaking her in, but she's a big dog and hard to miss, and the landlord warned me that if I got caught with a dog in my apartment, I'd get evicted. And I couldn't risk getting evicted after what we went through."

"Wow," sighed Victor, "how did you break the news to the kids?"

"It was terrible, almost as bad as telling them their daddy passed. They all cried and threw fits and resented me at first. Toi even volunteered to go to work, as young as she is, to earn extra money for a different apartment. But there was no choice, and I had to make the decision to place Rusty with a shelter that would guarantee me she wouldn't be euthanized. I even did research to find the most reputable place, so Rusty would get a good home. Even so, I never felt good about placing her in a shelter, and then a better option popped up. I told you how we used to walk Rusty around the neighborhood and how everyone loved her. Well, there was a man nearby who said he would take Rusty and give her a good home. This seemed like the perfect solution. I didn't know the man well, but I had often seen him in front of his house, tending to his garden or reading his tablet. He seemed friendly enough, and he'd occasionally pet Rusty, and she'd do one of her tricks for him. Anyway, I thought he'd be a better option than a shelter, and the kids agreed, so before we moved, we dropped her off at his house. We took her bed and her toys with us and gave him the dog food we still had left. Even so, it was hard to say goodbye to her. We loved that dog."

"Do you know the man's name?"

"No, not really. That sounds horrible, doesn't it? I think his first name was Ken or Carl… Carlton, that's it. His name was Carlton, but I don't know his last name."

"Do you know where he works?"

"No, I'm afraid not."

"Did he live on your street?"

"No, he owned a house just around the corner at 1704 Drexel Avenue."

"And as far as you know, he's still the dog's owner?"

"Yes, as far as I know. But I'd have no way of proving that."

Victor was satisfied that Larene had told him all she knew. "Thank you for sharing your story," he said as he rose to his feet. "You've been a big help."

"Wait, you never told me the details about what happened to Rusty. Is she okay?"

"Yes, she's okay. She was severely injured by someone, but she's currently recovering in the animal hospital. I think she's going to be fine."

"I'm glad to hear that. That dog deserves better than what she got. From what I could tell when she first showed up on our doorstep, she's had a rough time of it. I hope Carlton had nothing to do with hurting Rusty. I'd never forgive myself if that were the case."

"I don't know if he did, but I intend to find out. It's kind of become my mission in life."

"Well, I'm glad she's got you on her side. You seem like a nice man."

"Thank you," said Victor as he reached for the door. "Goodbye, Larene."

CHAPTER SIX

Victor had completed his morning exercise routine and was getting dressed for work. He walked into his closet and selected a pair of slacks and a clean shirt. The dress code for most workers at BioTech was business casual, but Victor was very particular about the way he dressed. He had a taste for expensive designer brands, and he favored tones in the blue and green spectrum. In that regard, he had something in common with Kyan Quantum, who favored similar colors and styles of clothing. He finished dressing and then sat down to eat an organic breakfast consisting of strawberry chia jam and eggs on toast with avocado and, of course, black coffee to drink. He had always preferred such breakfasts, although he had no idea why. He thought about the information he had acquired from Larene the night before and resolved to follow up on her lead as soon as time would allow. However, his workload at BioTech was growing exponentially, and he wasn't sure when he might be able to resume his search for the dog's owner.

Two hours later, while he was working feverishly at the lab, Romy-3 approached Victor and interrupted his concentration. "Victor, have you had a chance to run that voice simulator program I sent to you yesterday?"

"No, not yet. As per your directive, it is number three on my list of priorities."

"Well then, make it number one. Quinn needs it to move forward on his assignment."

"Why don't you just have Jericho run it?"

"Jericho has already run it. That's not enough; I need you to do it."

Victor, clearly annoyed, peeled away from his computer screen and glared at Romy-3. "I don't understand why everything needs to go through me. You sometimes act like I'm the only competent person working here."

"That's not true. Jericho and Quinn are excellent, but they aren't you." Romy-3 paused before continuing. "Victor, when I say that you possess a unique skill set that others simply cannot match, I'm not just trying to flatter you. Your expertise is unparalleled."

"Then perhaps I should mentor them and pass along this skill set. What if I were reassigned to Axle's team? What would you do then?"

"That's not likely to happen. I'm afraid you're stuck with me, like it or not."

But Victor had returned to working on his computer and was ignoring Romy-3.

"Victor, come into my office, please," she said as she walked away. Victor obediently followed her into her office, and they both took a seat at a small conference table placed adjacent to her desk.

"What's bothering you, Victor? Something is clearly on your mind besides work."

Victor stared into Romy-3's purple-colored eyes for a moment. "Romy, have you ever had a dog?" he said matter-of-factly.

She seemed confused. "Have I what?"

"Nothing. You asked what was on my mind."

Romy-3 seemingly paused to consider her next move. "Victor, do you know why I requested your transfer to my division? I mean, truly understand the logic behind it?"

"I guess you liked my work."

"Yes, I did, but that's not all of it. It's because

of who you are, or more specifically, *what* you are, that makes you uniquely qualified for what we do here. Your talents were being wasted on Axle's team. What they do over there is elementary compared to what we do here."

"I don't know. It seemed pretty important to me at the time."

"Yes, but it's on the periphery of the AI program. We are at the heart of it."

Victor still looked preoccupied and disengaged from Romy.

"You don't know what I'm talking about, do you, Victor?"

He didn't answer.

"Victor, describe yourself for me. Who are you?"

Now, she had his attention.

"I'm Victor X, telecommunication specialist at BioTech Industries."

"Okay, *what* are you?"

He stared at her.

"It's a serious question," she said.

He still just stared at her.

"Victor, I am going to tell you something about yourself you're not supposed to know, in fact, something that no one is supposed to know.

You are a humanoid, an android, to be exact. A very advanced android, the latest and greatest achievement of BioTech, Dr. Kyan Quantum's pet project."

Victor fell back in his chair. "What are you talking about? That's crazy; I don't believe you. You must be joking."

"But I'm not. I'm being forthright. Now, I'll tell you about me. I'm a robot, a female android, a gynoid. Except a much older version than you. You are the most advanced humanoid on planet Earth."

"Bullshit. This is preposterous. I'm made of flesh and blood, and I eat and drink like all humans."

"Because you were engineered that way. Our goal is to produce bio-hybrid humanoids who can assimilate into the human world without detection. Everything about you is designed to be as close to humanlike as possible, except more perfect. You eat and drink and even vacate waste product to support the biological aspect of your structure because you are programmed that way. You can have normal human sex. Hell, you can probably even procreate with a female human. But it's an illusion because, at the heart of it all, you are a machine. That's what our government contracts are all about and why they are worth so much money to BioTech."

Victor was left speechless, stunned by the revelation.

"Have I offended you?" she asked.

"Why?" he said curtly. "I'm a machine. I have no feelings."

"No," said Romy-3 as she rose and walked toward Victor, "*I* have no feelings, but you do. You were designed to be the perfect android. I have intelligence and strength and even a primitive capacity for creativity, but you have all that plus more, real feelings and emotions. I have been programmed to recognize what humans are feeling, when they are happy, sad, or excited. But you can actually feel those things, and that's what makes you so special, Victor. Right now, you are probably the most important person working at BioTech, and I need you on top of your game. Can you see now why you are so uniquely qualified to do the work that we do in the R&D lab?"

Victor was still in a state of disbelief, and all he could think of was getting the hell out of there. Suddenly, the atmosphere seemed contaminated, and it was hard to breathe. He needed fresh air, he needed space, and he needed something to ground himself to reality.

"Romy, I need to leave."

"Victor, wait…"

Victor rose from his chair. "No, Romy. I need to leave."

"Okay, I understand. But think about what I said, and I will see you tomorrow."

Victor left the office in a hurry, exiting the building and jumping into his car. He punched in coordinates, and the auto sped away, screeching its tires. There was only one place Victor could think of going to that would satisfy his need for feeling grounded. Negative thoughts were flooding through his brain from all directions as his car sped down the street toward his destination. This rage was a feeling he had never experienced before. "If I'm a fucking android, they must have done a damn good job of infusing me with feelings," he thought. He kept seeing Romy's stupefied face in his mind with her flat affect and her pasty white veneer. "She's a fucking robot, a gynoid," he thought. "No wonder she's such a bitch!"

Victor's car swung into the parking lot at the animal hospital, and he shut off the electric motor. He sat in silence for a moment of contemplation, frozen by the relentless assault on his consciousness. He looked down at his hands and turned them over and back again as if seeing them for the first time, and Romy's words were reverberating in his brain as if in an echo chamber. How could it be that he was not human, that he was a machine created and manufactured by humans? And yet that reality was sinking in, flooding his neurons with electrical impulses and forcing him to believe it was true. He exited the car and slowly walked into the hospital lobby just like he had done nearly every day for the prior two weeks, except now it was different.

"Hello, Mr. X. We were just talking about you," stated Marci cheerfully. "What is it that you do for BioTech?"

"I'm in telecommunications," said Victor as he approached the receptionist's desk.

"That's what I thought. One of my co-workers has a brother who used to work there. His name is Damian Brio, and he's a security guard."

"Hey, he's not a security guard," shouted an annoyed woman from across the room. "He works in security. There's a difference."

"Okay," laughed Marci, "he's in security, but now he works for Ross-Lear. Do you know him?"

"No. But a lot of people work at BioTech. It's a big company, and I haven't been there all that long."

"I see. Well, I was just wondering if you might know him. Anyway, you can take yourself back to the recovery room. You don't have to wait for a tech."

Victor nodded and walked swiftly through the door and into the hallway that led to the recovery room. There was still no sign of Dr. Zhang or any of the techs, so he entered the room and walked over to where Angel was sleeping. He examined her wounds and found they had healed remarkably well, such that other than the presence of the staples, she looked neatly put back together. Angel suddenly became aware of his presence, and she opened her eyes and immediately began wagging her tail.

"Hello Angel, did you have a good sleep?" he whispered to her.

Angel raised her head and began whimpering excitedly. Then, she slowly lifted her body to a standing position.

"Whoa, girl, I'm not sure you're supposed to do that," he said as he hugged and petted her.

"She's doing well," said Dr. Zhang as she entered the room. "Angel's been standing a little bit for the past few days. I think we can safely remove her staples, and you know what that means?"

"No, what?"

"She can go home! She'll have to stay on antibiotics for a few days as a precaution, but she's pretty much healed."

"And what does going home mean for Angel?" asked Victor.

"I don't know. Have you identified the owner yet?"

"Not exactly."

"Well, you know what I think? You would be the perfect person to take her home and nurse her back to health. She obviously loves you, and we send animals to foster homes all the time to aide them in their recovery. And should you eventually find the owner, you could reunite Angel with them later. What do you think?"

"I don't know...I suppose I could do that." Angel was gently nuzzling Victor's hand. "Can I think about it?"

"Of course. We'll remove the staples tomorrow and send her home with you if that's what you decide."

Victor continued petting Angel and speaking to her in soft, soothing tones. He traced her squiggly white line with his finger from her muzzle up to the top of her head and stared into her big brown eyes.

"I wonder what she sees when she looks into my eyes?" he thought to himself. "Does she know I'm a machine, or does she think I'm human?" Victor suddenly wondered what everyone else thinks when they look into his eyes. Do they see a human, or do they recognize the ruse? He thought back to what Romy-3 had said about him being the perfect android, capable of assimilating into the human world without detection. He hoped that was true because he hated admitting to himself that he was less than human, and the only thing worse was the thought that everyone else knew it, too. He even began to envy Angel. She was just a dog, but at least she was real, conceived and born into this world naturally and not the product of the R&D laboratory at BioTech. How many people participated in his creation, had their hands on him, or inside him? How many programmers worked on his software, wired his hard drive? Did Romy-3 help design him? She said that he was the pet project of Kyan Quantum, generally considered to be one of the most brilliant biomechanical engineers in the world. Does that make Quantum, in essence, Victor's father? Is it even relevant to speak of progeny for an android? Victor was suddenly feeling all alone in the world, a one-of-a-kind freak, grounded to nothing. He hugged Angel tightly, and she licked his face, and he felt her rough, wet tongue, and he smelled her sweet breath, and a comforting feeling washed over his mien. "How could I not be human," he wondered?

"Mr. X...Mr. X, are you alright?" asked Dr. Zhang.

"Yes, I'm alright. I guess I'll go now. I'll let you know tomorrow what I've decided to do. Goodbye, Angel."

Victor left the animal hospital and drove home, choosing a protracted route to allow for more time to process his thoughts. He plugged the coordinates into his autonomous navigation system and sat back in his seat. He then picked up his computer tablet and researched the name of Kyan Quantum. According to Quantum's profile, he went to school at Stanford University, where he began his career studying medicine, intending to be a physician. However, he switched disciplines and later received his Master of Science degree in Biomechanical Engineering and eventually acquired a PhD in Bioengineering. He was a proud member of Alpha Eta Mu Beta, the Bioengineering Honor Society, and had graduated at the top of his class. Quantum was one of the most highly sought-after bioengineers in the world when BioTech landed him as their CEO fifteen years prior, and he was largely responsible for the company's prestige as the leader in artificial intelligence technology. Quantum was married to Lillian Quantum and had two children, Argon and Tully.

Victor shut off his tablet, rested his head back in his seat, and closed his eyes. "So, this is who made me, my creator," he thought to himself. Quantum certainly had the credentials, but that in itself was an insulting thought, as if humans ever questioned the credentials of their creator. Victor's electric car wound its way through the city streets, and he would occasionally glance over into the adjacent vehicles when stopped at a traffic light, wondering if any of the occupants were humanoids like him and, if so, what dark thoughts might they hold in their minds. His car eventually made it home and parked itself in the garage. He hopped out and made his way into his apartment, his mind still whirring with activity. But for the first time, there were no calculations to be made that could answer his questions, no data to scrutinize that might clarify things. He picked up a pan and reflexively began preparing dinner, an activity he now realized was driven more by program than necessity, and he suddenly had no appetite. He threw down the pan in disgust and accidentally splashed liquid on his shirt. He exited the kitchen and retired to the living room, where he requested classical music from his virtual assistant. He sat down in his favorite easy chair and closed his eyes in an attempt to induce a meditative state, but even that offered little relief. There was now an unquenchable thirst for information engulfing his being, and he felt the need to speak to someone. But to whom could he speak of such things as were plaguing his mind? Who could possibly understand his dilemma, appreciate his angst? Axle. Axle might understand. He needed to call Axle.

CHAPTER SEVEN

The phone rang.

"Hello, Victor. What's up?"

"Hello, Axle. I need to see you this evening if possible."

"Sure. Is it work related?"

"Kind of."

"Okay. Do you want to meet me somewhere or just come over to the house?"

"Your house would be fine. Have you finished with dinner?"

"Yes, I have. Come on over."

"Alright. See you shortly."

Victor ended the call and went into his bedroom to put on a clean shirt. He then jumped back into his car and made the short drive to Axle's house, which was located in an exclusive subdivision above the city. There were a lot of questions on his mind, and Victor was mentally preparing himself for this critical discussion. He parked his car in front of Axle's home, a slickly designed modern bungalow featuring lots of chrome and tinted glass. He ran up to the door and announced his presence to the security system. A laser scanned him, and then the door opened to reveal Axle standing in the vestibule.

"Hello, Victor, come on in. Have you met my wife, Maggie?"

"No, I have not. Hello Maggie. I'm Victor."

"Good to meet you," she said pleasantly as she offered him her hand. "Why don't you guys go into the family room, and I'll bring you some drinks if you'd like."

"No, nothing for me," said Victor. "But thanks for offering."

"Nothing for now, babe," said Axle as he kissed her on the cheek. "Follow me, Victor."

Victor followed Axle down the short hallway and into a spacious family room. There were large windows along one entire wall, providing a spectacular view of the city below. The room featured neutral color tones of gray and black, and there was an el-shaped sectional in the middle of the room. A billiard table was strategically placed to the right of the sectional, and a wet bar along the opposing wall.

"I love your house," said Victor as he surveyed his surroundings.

"Thanks. Have a seat." Victor sat at one end of the sectional, Axle at the other. "Now, what can I do for you?"

"Axle, do you consider yourself to be my friend?"

"Of course."

"I don't just mean a work friend, but a friend in the general sense of the word."

"Yes, I should like to think so."

"And, therefore, you can be totally honest with me?"

"Sure."

"And if I told you something in strict confidence, would you maintain my trust?"

"Yes, I would. Victor, is this about work?"

"I'm getting to that. Axle, I have reason to believe that I'm different from everybody else."

"Different? In what way, Victor?"

"In every way. You see, I think I'm a bio-hybrid humanoid."

"Whaaat?" said Axle incredulously.

"You know, an android with flesh and

blood."

"I know what a bio-hybrid is. But you're joking, right? I mean, you're not being serious."

"Yes, Axle, I am."

Axle sat still and stared at Victor for a moment. "So, this is what was plaguing you? I think I can explain your feelings. Victor, there is a psychological phenomenon common to those of us who work in the field of artificial intelligence, where we identify so closely with AI that we start to wonder if we might be one ourselves. I've seen this happen before, and it's quite normal."

"No, Axle, that's not it at all. This isn't like counter-projection in psychology. I have some excellent reasons to believe I'm an android. Do you know anything about that?"

Axle rose from his seat, looking quite disturbed. "You know, I think I will have a drink after all. Can I get you one?" he asked as he walked to the wet bar.

"No thanks."

Axle poured himself a bourbon on the rocks and then stopped to stare out the window. "You know, this view is one of the reasons why we bought this house. Hell, it may be the main reason."

"You're being evasive, Axle. You haven't

answered my question."

Axle spun around and walked back to the sectional. "No, I haven't, have I? You're not going to let this go, are you, Victor?"

"No, I'm not."

Axle heaved a deep sigh and then sipped from his glass. "Why are you asking me this, Victor? Did someone else already discuss this with you?"

"Yes."

"Who?"

"Romy-3."

"Shit," whispered Axle, realizing there was no point in continuing to deny. "I'm sorry you had to find out like this. You're right. You are a bio-hybrid humanoid. But I'm not supposed to tell you that, and you're not supposed to know. I...we *all* were sworn to secrecy. There is an awful lot riding on your existence, Victor. If you only knew."

"I think I do know, but I appreciate you finally telling me the truth, even if I had to drag it out of you. But why? Why create the 'perfect android' and then keep it a secret from me?"

"I'm afraid that's way above my pay grade, Victor."

"Who else knows at BioTech? Is my status common knowledge?"

"No, not at all. This has been a carefully guarded secret. Only a few select division heads were informed, and we were threatened with termination if we exposed the truth. We went to great lengths to protect your identity, like fabricating your resume, making you apply for your own position, and requiring everybody in your division to undergo those monthly doctor exams in order to justify getting you to the clinic to run AI diagnostics. We couldn't have you thinking that you were being treated any differently than the others."

"But I have childhood memories about my adolescence and graduating from college…"

"All planted in your memory banks, programmed into your software. Victor, you literally came online just before coming to work at BioTech three years ago. Anything you remember before that is an illusion; it never happened."

"Fascinating. Tell me, why did I get transferred to Romy-3?"

"Why? Because you're a fucking genius. And your very existence makes you uniquely qualified to write software code and identify flaws in robotic systems. It was a logical extension of your work duties."

"What about Romy-3? She told me who she was. Does everyone know about her?"

"Romy-3 has been around a long time. She's an earlier version of you. I think a lot of people suspect it, but it's never been outright confirmed. Quantum is very particular about his android workforce, and if he can't pass them off as humans to his own people, how can he convince the government of the veracity of the project? Ironically, once it became fashionable for many humans to reduce their last names to a single letter or digit, it was easier for Quantum to name his hybrids. I heard him say one time that your name, Victor X, was meant to be a veiled reference to the term deus ex machina. You know, like Victor ex machina."

"*God from the machine.* Should I be flattered?"

"Well, let us just say that humility is not a strong point of Quantum's. As far as Romy-3 is concerned, in order to plant the seeds of doubt about her true status, Quantum developed an impressive personnel portfolio for her and even supported rumors about her wild personal life. He made sure she was seen often in public with some of his eligible bachelor friends, and even on occasion with eligible females."

"But if all of you were sworn to secrecy, why

do you think that Romy-3 told me who I really am?"

"That I can't answer, Victor. She must have her reasons. But I can tell you this, Quantum won't be happy."

Victor rose from his seat and walked toward the billiard table. "I think I will have a drink, Axle."

"Okay. What would you like?"

"Whatever you're having."

Axle poured another bourbon on the rocks and refreshed his own drink while Victor prepared to fire a break shot. After scattering the balls, he moved adroitly around the table and ran the rack cleanly, making a variety of difficult cut shots and combinations along the way, greatly impressing Axle.

"Holy shit, Victor. I should take you on the road. We could make a fortune from your billiard skills."

"I guess that's a perk of being an android: having perfect eye-hand coordination and the ability to calculate angles precisely."

Axle handed Victor his glass of bourbon. "Cheers," he said, as they both sipped from their drinks. "I hope this doesn't affect our friendship."

"Really? I can assure you from my perspective, it won't, or I wouldn't be here right now. But I have another unrelated question to ask."

"Okay. Shoot."

"Do you know anything about that dog I found injured on the side of the road?"

"You mean other than what you've told me? No. Why?"

"Never mind. I'm probably just chasing shadows. Do you want to play a game of billiards?"

"Sure. You'll probably kick my ass, but why not. I'll rack 'em up."

Victor and Axle played a best of five series, which Victor won easily with a score of 3-1. However, Axle was convinced that Victor threw one game so he wouldn't get shut out on his own table.

"Well, I should be going, Axle. Thanks for meeting with me tonight, and I promise not to betray your confidence."

"You're welcome, Victor. Look, I'm truly sorry you had to find out this way. But as to our earlier discussion, let me reiterate, I will always remain your friend, regardless of the circumstances."

"Thanks, Axle," said Victor as they shook hands. "I appreciate that. Goodbye."

The drive home was slow, dark, and lonely,

and Victor tried hard to purge his mind of any
thoughts regarding his creation. He was tired of
contemplation and simply longing for a restful
escape from what was plaguing him. "God damn
them for creating me," he thought, "and God damn
them for making me feel like this."

The following workday at BioTech was
initially unremarkable. Everyone around Victor
seemed to have returned to normal as if nothing
had changed. Romy-3 was back to being a hard-
ass taskmaster, Jericho joked around with Victor
like he always did, and when Victor ran into him
in the hallway, Axle acted like the conversation
from the night before had never happened. They
were the same, but for Victor, things were quite
different now. He saw the world from a whole new
perspective, and it tainted everything he touched.
How could it not? Now, when he ran simulations
or wrote software code, he imagined it being done
with him in mind or with others just like him. It felt
uncommonly relevant and horrifyingly prescient
regarding his future. To calm himself, he imagined
as if he were a human physician working on a cure
for a disease he himself had contracted. However,
this was a fallacious analogy, for he doubted
anyone on the human side ever tried the reverse,

to imagine themselves as an android when solving a design problem. What did the humans know, or even care, what it was like to be him?

However, the most important decision to be made on that day was unrelated to work. This was the day that Angel would be eligible to be released from the hospital, but before Victor would go there, he had another stop to make. He keyed 1704 Drexel Avenue into the navigator and made the drive to Larene's old neighborhood. He pulled up in front of the house, which was an old last-century structure, built with a brick façade and featuring a stately oak tree planted squarely in the middle of the lawn. The car shut down, and he sat there for a second, looking for any signs of activity. He exited the auto, walked slowly up the hill to the front door, and rang the old-school doorbell. By that time, it was quite unusual to still find a homeowner without a sophisticated security system for monitoring trespassers. There was no immediate answer, so Victor rang the bell again, and this time, a man opened the door.

"Hello. My name is Victor X. Are you Carlton?"

"Yes. What's this about?"

"I received your name and address from Larene Langston. Can we talk?"

"I don't know any Larene Langston," said the man as he started to close the door.

"Yes, you do, the woman who gave you your dog, Rusty."

"Oh, her. Yeah, I know her. What do you want?"

"I just want to ask you a few questions, that's all. Can I come in?"

"Look, Mack, I don't know you from Adam, and I got nothing to say to you about my dog. So, why don't you just get off my porch."

Again, the man started to close the door, but Victor stopped it with his hand. "I'm not leaving until you answer a few questions."

The man pushed on the door again, but this time, Victor forced his way into the house and threw the man against the wall. "Listen, *Mack*, I'm not leaving here without some answers. Unfortunately, you've caught me in a bad mood, so I suggest you cooperate."

"Alright, alright, chill out. What do you want to know?"

"Where's your dog?"

"I don't know. She's around here somewhere."

"What do you mean 'somewhere'? Is she in

the house?"

"No."

"In the yard?"

"No."

"The neighborhood?"

"I don't know, I guess so," he said with a cocky attitude.

Victor pushed the man against the wall again and lifted him off the ground. "What did you do with Rusty?"

"Hang on, no need to get rough. I sold her."

Victor let the man down. "Sold her to whom and when?"

"To this guy I know, about two or three weeks ago."

"Does this guy have a name?"

"I only know him as Rowdy. We frequent the same bar."

"Which bar?"

"The Blue Sky."

"And what do you know about this *Rowdy* character?"

"Not much. He's a cheap hood, a punk, a gopher. He picks up a few bucks here and there by helping out."

"Really. Why did you sell the dog to Rowdy?

I thought you liked her and promised to give her a good home?"

"I do like her. She's a great dog, friendly, obedient. But the dude offered me five hundred bucks cash for her. I figured he must want that dog pretty bad for that kind of money, and I couldn't pass up a chance like that. I got bills to pay."

"Did he tell you why he wanted the dog so badly?"

"Not exactly, but I thought it was weird for Rowdy to flash that kind of money around. He said it was for some rich dude at BioTech."

"BioTech?" said Victor incredulously.

"Yeah, that big tech company across town. You ever heard of it?"

"Yeah, I've heard of it. Anything else? Did he mention a name for his contact at BioTech?"

"No, that was all he said, some rich dude. And I didn't ask."

Victor grabbed the man's shirt with both fists and started to lift him off the ground again.

"No, please, I'm telling you the truth," he squealed. "I don't know who he was working for."

Victor let go and started to walk away.

"Hey mister, why all the questions? You a cop or something?"

"Not a cop, but something. Have a good evening, Carlton."

Victor left the house and walked back down the hill to his car. It was time to go see Angel, and now he had a clearer picture of her future. His car slowly wove its way through the rush hour traffic and delivered him to the vet hospital. Victor hopped out and strutted through the entrance into the lobby, still hot from his confrontation with Carlton.

"Hello, Mr. X," said Marci.

Victor ignored her greeting and walked silently over to the coffee maker and poured himself a cup of black coffee.

"I said, hello, Mr. X."

"Oh, hello, Marci," he said.

"This is the big day, huh? Angel finally gets to go home."

"Yes, this is the big day. Is Dr. Zhang here?"

"Yes, she's here. I'll tell her you've arrived."

Besides Victor, there was only one other pet owner in the lobby, an elderly woman sitting patiently in the corner reading a magazine. One of the techs suddenly emerged from the back room with the woman's little dog in tow, who had been boarding at the hospital while she was away for the weekend. "Oh, there's my little baby," exclaimed the woman as she set down the magazine and rose from her seat. "I hope you were a good girl."

"Dolly was a delight, Mrs. H. We always love having her stay with us."

"Oh, thank you," she said as she took the leash from the tech. "Do I owe you anything?"

"No, ma'am. You're all paid up."

"Oh, good. Come on, Dolly, let's go home."

Just then, Dr. Zhang appeared in the lobby. "Hello, Mr. X. Please tell me you have decided to take Angel home with you."

"Yes, I have."

"Oh, that makes me so happy! We removed her staples this morning, and she has healed nicely. The surgical site looks clean and healthy."

"That's good to hear. I want to update you on what I've learned about her ownership. I was able to trace her history through five different owners, the last one taking possession of her about three weeks ago, just before she was injured. Some guy named Rowdy bought her for five hundred dollars from the guy Larene Langston gave the dog to. Oh, and Angel has had a number of names, but I found out she was last known as Rusty."

"What about the person who cut her? Do

you think Rowdy is the one who did it?"

"I can't say for sure, but it's a good bet. I have one more string to pull, and I should get the answer. But I'm not prepared to discuss that yet."

"Okay. Keep me posted, and I'll add it to my police report when the time comes. As for right now, I'm so glad that you have decided to take Angel — or Rusty — home with you."

"Yes, I definitely want to do that. After what I've discovered about her history, I can't imagine placing her with yet another person."

"That's excellent. We have her all cleaned up and ready to go. I'll have Kyree bring her out to you while I go get her medicine."

"Dr. Zhang, do I owe you any money?"

"Mr. X, you don't owe us a thing. We received your very generous donation the other day. That, and your kindness to Angel, is more than enough for us."

Dr. Zhang disappeared, and Kyree entered the waiting area with Angel tethered to a leash and walking closely by her side. It was the first time Victor had actually seen her walk since he rescued her. Emotions welled up inside him as he stooped down to hug the dog. "Rusty, look at you walking around like normal!" The dog whimpered excitedly and nuzzled Victor as he petted her head. Just then, Dr. Zhang reappeared with the dog's medicine, and Victor reached out to take the bag. "She looks great, doc! Thank you so much for all you've done for her. I really didn't think she would survive that ordeal."

"I know, it's one of the worst cases I have ever seen, but she has a big heart and a fighting spirit. And your persistent friendship during her recovery played a large part. Don't ever underestimate that."

Victor tried to shake hands with the staff, but Dr. Zhang, Kyree, and Marci would have none of it. They each insisted on hugging Victor, and tears of joy and gratitude were shed that day in the hospital lobby. Victor and Rusty said goodbye, and Victor led her out the door and into the parking lot, gently lifting her and placing her into the backseat of his car. "What do you say, Rusty? You ready to go home?"

CHAPTER EIGHT

Victor was close to finding out who was responsible for Rusty's attack, and somebody at BioTech was connected. But who? It wasn't likely that the street thug named Rowdy would shell out five hundred dollars just to mutilate a dog, so the person at BioTech must have cooked it up. But why? Victor needed a name, someone to connect the dots to, and he needed it badly. Even his celebrated ability to focus on his assignments at work was being impugned, and he wouldn't have any peace until he unearthed this final fact.

Victor decided to pay a visit to the Blue Sky Bar to see what he might discover. It was a crusty little neighborhood establishment, a greasy burger and beer joint, that attracted mostly locals after work and a few stragglers during the day. It featured a big blue neon sign above the entrance, which, on the night that Victor was there, was only half-lit. He took a seat at the bar and ordered a beer from the gregarious female bartender.

"You're not one of my regulars, are you?"

"No. It's my first time here."

"Do you live in this neighborhood?"

"No, but I have some friends that do."

"I thought you looked too classy for my typical crowd," she joked as she used a rag to wipe down the bar top.

"What's that supposed to mean?"

"Oh, I meant no offense. It's just that most of my customers are manual laborers or on government subsidies."

"Then yeah, I'm not your typical patron," said Victor as he gulped down half of his beer.

"Just the same. You're as welcome here as anybody else. In fact, I like to see a clean-cut man like you every now and then."

"Speaking of your regular patrons, do you know a guy named Rowdy who supposedly hangs out here?"

"Rowdy? No, that name doesn't ring a bell. I might know him if I saw him, but the name is unfamiliar." The bartender yelled down at the man sitting at the end of the bar. "Hey, Flynn. You know a guy named Rowdy from around here?"

"No, can't say that I do," mumbled the man as he took a drag from his cigarette.

"Ah, you're no help," she said as she hung the bar rag on a towel rack.

Victor pulled out a pen and a small piece of paper from his pocket. "I'll tell you what, if you figure out who this guy is, I'd appreciate it if you'd let me know."

The woman picked up the piece of paper and studied the information. "Victor X, huh? Alright, Mr. X, I'll keep my eyes open."

"Thanks," he said as he gulped down the rest of his beer and tossed some money on the bar. "You never know. There might even be a reward in it for you."

Victor started to exit the bar, and the bartender placed the cash into the till. He glanced back and saw her crumble up the paper and throw it into the trashcan. He thought about going back and asking why, but he already knew the answer.

In order to provide better care for Rusty, Victor requested and received permission to work from home for a while. The arrangement proved to be advantageous for both Victor and the dog. During the first forty-eight hours after returning home with Victor, Rusty mostly just slept in the bed he had prepared for her in one of the spare bedrooms. She seemed comfortable and well on the road to a full recovery from her nasty wound, and Victor found it easier to focus on his work with Rusty resting just a few feet away. The animal hospital had been making daily phone calls to check on the dog's progress, and one of those calls proved to be fortuitous for Victor.

"Hello, Mr. X, this is Marci at the pet hospital."

"Hello Marci."

"How is our patient doing today?"

"She's doing fine. Her appetite has improved, and she's moving around more freely each day, although she's asleep in her bed right now."

"That's good to hear. She's probably still a little sore, but she'll be as good as new in no time. I just wanted to check on her."

"Hey Marci, while I have you on the phone, I have a question about your co-worker's brother, the guy who works in security at Ross-Lear."

"You mean Damian Brio?"

"That's right. Have you ever met Mr. Brio?"

"No, can't say that I have. He's Jaylen's brother, you know, the tech who cleans up around here. But I don't think he's ever been to the office. You remember Jaylen, don't you?"

"Yes, I think so. Thanks for the information, Marci. I may look up Mr. Brio sometime."

"You're welcome. Have a good day, and don't hesitate to call us if you need anything."

Victor sat down at the computer terminal and searched through the Ross-Lear website to see if he could find the employee contact information. Sure enough, it was there, and he discovered Brio wasn't just some guy in security. He was the deputy to the company's Chief Security Officer (CSO) and the person primarily in charge of risk reduction. Victor was developing a plan for trying to identify Rowdy's connection to BioTech. He was afraid that if he started snooping around the company hierarchy himself, they would just shut him down before he ever found out who ordered the hit on Rusty. So instead of that, he thought about enlisting the help of Damian Brio. But he needed a little more information before making that move. So, later that evening, he contacted Lacy, his neighborhood friend and tennis partner, who also happened to work at Ross-Lear.

"Hello, Victor. What's up? You're not calling to back out of our tennis match this weekend, are you?"

"No, not at all. Margo and I look forward to trouncing you and Kelm on the tennis courts again. I'm calling about something entirely different, something work-related. Do you happen to know a guy named Damien Brio at Ross-Lear?"

"No, but I haven't been there that long. What does he do?"

"Deputy CSO over risk reduction."

"Oh, well, I barely know the names of all the people in my own tech division. Why do you ask?"

"I can't give you all the details right now, but I need to know if he's trustworthy. Would you mind looking into it and getting back to me in the next twenty-four hours? It's really important."

"Oh, some cool spy shit! Okay, I'll get you an answer by tomorrow. But then you owe me, Victor."

"Okay, I'll spot you and Kelm three games next time instead of the customary two."

"That's not exactly what I had in mind, Victor. But okay, it's a deal."

The next day, Victor received a text message from Lacy, which simply read: *"Brio is a boy scout. His word is his bond."* Armed with that information, Victor forged ahead with his plan and left Brio a voice message. One hour later, he received a call back.

"Is this Victor X?"

"Yes, it is."

"This is Damian Brio returning your call."

"Hello, Damian. Thanks for calling me back."

"Not a problem. So, you say you work at BioTech, right?"

"Yes, in the R&D lab. Do you know Romy-3?"

"Yeah, I remember her. Is she your boss?"

"She is. When did you leave BioTech?"

"Ah, let's see…about three years ago. I got a better offer at Ross-Lear and took the plunge. I think I pissed off a lot of people over there at BioTech. They don't like losing employees to their competitor."

"I know what you mean. Let me get to the point. I have something important to discuss with you, but I'd prefer if we do it outside of work, if that's okay."

"Alright, I guess so. Where do you suggest?"

"There's a farmer's market on the north side of town near the museum. Do you know what I'm talking about?"

"Yes, I know the place."

"How about we meet there tomorrow at noon? There's a wine shop near the main entrance. We could meet there."

"Okay, that works for me. I'll call you when I arrive."

"Sounds good. See you then."

Victor ended the call and immediately felt something cold and wet rubbing his arm. "Hello, Rusty! I see you've wakened from your nap," he said as he petted her head. The dog barked softly and walked toward the door. "Oh, I see. You need to use the bathroom, don't you? Alright, let's go outside for a walk."

Victor rose from his chair and led Rusty outside. It was a beautiful sunny afternoon with high skies and a mild temperature, and he spent the next half hour walking her around the apartment complex. Rusty seemed to enjoy the exercise, but Victor noticed how she favored her injured side. Dr. Zhang had assured him it would gradually get better over time as the dog regained her strength, but the sight of it angered Victor and cemented his resolve to hold someone accountable for her mutilation.

The following afternoon, Victor drove to

the farmer's market for his meeting with Brio. He waited outside the wine shop until he received a phone call.

"Victor, this is Damian. I'm walking through the entrance right now, and I can see the wine shop."

"Great. I'm standing outside the store, wearing a light green shirt."

"I see you. I'll be right there."

As Brio approached, Victor sized him up. He was a tall man, probably in his mid-thirties, with dark skin, a stocky build, and a professional demeanor. At first glance, he seemed like the kind of person you could trust. When he arrived at where Victor was standing, Brio offered him his hand. "Hello, Victor. Damian Brio."

"Good to meet you, Damian. There's a great deli just around the corner. Let's grab a sandwich and take a seat outside."

They made their way to the deli and placed their orders.

"I appreciate you meeting with me. I don't think I mentioned how I got your name. You apparently have a sister who works at the animal hospital, right?"

"Yes, my sister Jaylen. I have another sister

named Karma, who works at a local bank. How do you know Jaylen?"

They were abruptly interrupted by a deli employee who yelled out, "To go order for Victor."

"Excuse me, I'll grab our sandwiches," said Victor to Brio. Then, they walked outside and took a seat at a picnic table.

"Okay, you asked me how I know Jaylen. I had an extremely sick dog at the animal hospital where she works, and the subject just came up in casual conversation since she knew I worked at BioTech."

"I see. I'm sorry about your dog. Is she or he okay now?"

"Yes, she's doing fine now. But she was severely injured and almost died."

"Some kind of an accident?"

"No, an intentional and brutal attack. Someone tried to skin her alive."

"Holy shit! You're kidding me," exclaimed Brio. "That's disgusting. I'm a dog owner myself, I have a Great Dane, and it angers me to hear stuff like that. Who would do such a despicable thing, and how the hell does a dog survive that kind of an attack?"

"She was left on the side of the road,

and I discovered her while cycling around my neighborhood. I couldn't get anyone else to help, so I went home, got my car, and took her to the hospital."

"Wait a minute, I thought she was your dog?"

"No, not at the time I found her. I didn't know who she belonged to, but I was committed to discovering both who owned her and who assaulted her."

"And were you able to answer those questions?"

"No. I did trace her ownership through five different parties, but I'm still in the process of answering the other question. And that brings me to you and why we're having this meeting."

"I don't understand...how could I possibly be of any help? Did you notify the authorities?"

"Yes, the hospital took care of that, but so far, they've been unresponsive. Damian, I think you might be in a unique position to assist me. You see, the last person to own Rusty—that's the dog's name—was some street punk named Rowdy who bought her for five hundred dollars, supposedly for 'some rich dude' at BioTech, whatever that means. Because of my status as a current employee, I thought that if I started asking questions, everyone would clam up, and I'd never figure out the connection. But you, as a former employee associated with security, might have a better chance of unearthing the truth."

Brio finished eating his sandwich and wiped his face clean with his napkin. "Victor, this is a bizarre story. But I must admit it intrigues me. Are you suggesting there's a cover-up going on within the hierarchy at BioTech?"

"Yes, I believe I am," said Victor as he sipped from his drink.

"But why? What could possibly be the motivation for mutilating an animal like that and then covering it up?"

"I don't know."

"And you want me to poke around discreetly and figure out who the rich dude is. Victor, there are a lot of rich dudes at BioTech."

"I know, I'm asking a lot of you to poke your nose into their business."

"It's not just that. I do have a full-time job, you know. But on the other hand, now that I'm with Ross-Lear, if I could uncover some damaging information about BioTech, that wouldn't be such a bad thing. You see, before I left, I had been passed over for promotion several times, and I was basically stuck at my then current position. The Ross-Lear gig was a step up both in title and salary, and I wasn't going to let that slip away. BioTech tried to stop me from taking the job by evoking a non-compete clause, but I found a way to beat them at their own game. I told you I pissed off a lot of people over there."

"Then, you'll help me?"

Damian paused and stared into Victor's eyes for a moment. "Yes, I believe I will. I'll have to give this some thought to figure out the best way to approach the situation. But yeah, I'm in."

"Excellent! Shall we drink to it? I mean, it's just iced tea, but it'll have to do."

Victor and Brio raised their cups and drank to their new partnership.

"So, how do you like working for Romy-3?" asked Brio.

"It's...interesting. Some people find her management style objectionable, but I find her to be intelligent and a good leader."

"You do know what she is, right?"

"What do you mean?"

"She's a gynoid, a female android. You knew that, right?"

"Oh, that. Yes, I knew that. Although, it's not supposed to be common knowledge."

"Ha! I could tell the first time I met her. She's well built, don't get me wrong. But I can tell the difference between a human and a humanoid. I bet you can, too, working in the R&D lab."

Victor smiled and looked away for a moment. "Yes, I suppose you're right."

"Well, I've got to get going," said Brio as he rose from his seat. "I'm running late for a meeting. I'll be in touch."

Victor rose up and shook hands with Brio. "Thanks, Damian. I look forward to hearing back from you."

CHAPTER NINE

Rusty was getting stronger every day, and Victor no longer felt the need to stay home with her. Now that she was living with him, Victor was able to see firsthand what a remarkable dog she really was. She was attentive and obedient and possessed an expansive understanding of verbal commands. Now that her wounds were healed, he could take her outside and run her hard by tossing a ball in the courtyard. Her increased visibility and friendly demeanor made her the favorite dog in the apartment complex, and the residents loved to pet her and play fetch with her until her big pink tongue was dragging on the ground. She was especially sweet with the children, sitting quietly while they learned how to properly pet a dog, and she patiently tolerated the occasional pulled ear or overzealous hug around the neck. It made Victor think back to what he had learned from Larene about how quickly her kids took to Rusty and how they had used her as a nanny pet. It was a shame how things turned out, or the dog would likely still be with the Langstons.

In the weeks immediately following his meeting with Damian Brio, Victor was able to refocus his energy on work-related projects and less on his search for Rusty's attacker. His workload at BioTech was ramping up, as Romy-3 made him the point of contact for developing high-level software management platform intelligence that could deploy, operationalize, and monitor bots reliably. Romy's team had developed monitoring visualization tools but looked to Victor to help customize these tools for individual business units. Besides being a technological challenge, the development of software bots also needed to consider variables such as human sentiment and the nuances of language. Victor was in a unique position to focus on these important aspects of bot development, and Romy pushed him to take full advantage of his skills. Victor responded favorably to her challenge, and the R&D division of BioTech Industries had never been more productive. For the moment, at least, Victor was at peace with the state of his existence until one evening after work, while outside playing with Rusty, he received another call from Damian Brio.

"Victor, do you have a second to talk?"

"Sure, go ahead."

"I've made a breakthrough in my investigation. You said the last person to own the dog was some punk named Rowdy, right?"

"Yes, that's correct."

"Alright, I talked to a friend of mine in security at BioTech, and he recognized the name as belonging to a guy who visited the office a couple of times about a month ago. He signed in as Rowdy Ziris, and he hasn't been back since then. You're never going to guess who he was there to see."

"I assume it was someone in upper management."

"You could say that, about as high up as you can get. He was there to see Dr. Quantum."

"Quantum? Are you sure?"

"Yes, my friend was sure that the guy was there to see Quantum. He remembered it because Rowdy didn't look like the kind of person who would have business with Quantum. So, I looked up the guy's police record. Turns out, he's a street thug with a long rap sheet for numerous petty crimes, but he does have two felonies, one for aggravated assault, and get this: one charge from two years ago for felony animal cruelty."

Victor was momentarily left speechless. "This is perplexing. I thought that once you discovered the connection at BioTech, the mystery would be solved, but this just adds another layer to the dilemma. Why would Dr. Quantum hire a street thug like Rowdy to mutilate a dog?"

"Let's back it up, Victor. Who did Rowdy buy the dog from? Maybe Quantum was sending a message to that person."

"Some guy named Carlton, but I can't imagine any connection between him and Dr. Quantum."

"Then I don't know. I can keep nosing around if you want me to. I might come up with something else. Who knows?"

"Yes, please stay on the trail, Damian. Thanks for the info."

"No problem. I'll stay in touch."

The news that Quantum was somehow linked to Rowdy Ziris was troubling to Victor and certainly needed to be addressed, but he was momentarily lost for ideas. In the meantime, things were happening at work that would prove to have a significant impact on Victor's future. On Wednesday of the following week, Romy-3 was invited to make a presentation to the core leadership team regarding the latest achievements generated by the R&D lab, and she chose to highlight Victor's work in software robotics. Later that same day, Victor ran into Axle, who was just returning from lunch.

"Hey Victor, I want you to know that you garnered a ton of accolades at the core leadership meeting this morning."

"Really?"

"Hell, yes. Romy-3 showed us your latest work with the software bots, and if I didn't know any better, I'd swear she was bragging. You know, because she's not supposed to feel any emotions."

"Yeah, I get it, Axle. However, Romy-3 has keen observational skills and is good at imitating human behavior."

Axle laughed and patted Victor on the back. "Imitating human behavior, that's a good one. There are stories I could tell you, my friend, but I digress. She wasn't the only one bragging over you. You should have heard Quantum. I swear, the way he gushed over your productivity was just like a proud papa. I'm sure you'll be hearing something directly from him soon, or at least you should."

"Thanks, Axle. I appreciate you relaying that information. But I'm late for a meeting with Quinn and Jericho, so you'll have to excuse me."

"Yeah, sure, buddy. Hey, we need to go out for drinks after work sometime soon so you can catch me up on what's going on in your life."

"Sounds good. I'll see you later."

It was Friday of that same week when Damian contacted Victor with more information from his investigation. Victor was at his desk working on a new assignment when Brio called.

"Victor, I hate to bother you at work, but I just received some information that I thought you needed to hear."

"Okay, go ahead."

"I just spoke to a connection of mine in the BioTech finance department, and she tells me that Quantum made a six-thousand-dollar payment to Rowdy Ziris about a month ago for 'services rendered.' The fact that she was privy to this information tells me two things: One, he didn't try to hide the payment, and two, this expenditure was somehow perceived as company business. Victor, this gets us probably as close as we're ever going to get to proving that Quantum was responsible for ordering that hit on your dog. The only thing we don't know is why, and we might never know the answer to that question without asking him directly. There may be only one or two people in the entire company, if that, who know the truth."

Victor did not respond at once to Brio's report.

"Victor, are you still there? Did you hear what I said?"

"Yes, I heard you, Damian."

"I know this must be a big disappointment for you, considering he's your CEO and the foremost bioengineer in the country. In fact, as much as they despise him, the people at Ross-Lear would give anything to lure him over to their side. But everyone knows Dr. Quantum is arrogant and tightly wound, the epitome of the genius playboy. Who knows what the fuck is going on in his mind? Maybe he's snapped, or maybe he's bored. But then, probably nobody appreciates his technical savvy more than you."

"What do you mean by that?" asked Victor defensively.

"You know, because of your work with Romy-3. You guys are right at the heart of the AI program, and that's where the big money is and the most carefully guarded secrets."

"Damian, do you plan on using any of this information against BioTech?"

"I wish I could. But I don't have enough proof to publicly vilify Quantum. But I do have enough information to lurk in the weeds and see if he makes a mistake. I'll keep my eyes and ears open, and if I learn anything more, I'll let you know."

"Sounds good. I greatly appreciate all that you've done for me, Damian. Someday, we'll have to figure out how I can pay you back."

"Forget it, Victor. I've got to admit it was a pleasant diversion from my regular job. And don't forget, I'm a dog guy, too. Catch you later."

Victor tried to return to his work on the computer, but he was distracted by the image of Kyan Quantum floating in his head. He stared into the screen, and there was Quantum. He looked away at the wall, and there was Quantum. He rose from his chair and walked over to the coffee machine, poured a cup of black coffee, and there was Quantum again, staring back at him through a reflection in the dark liquid. He set the coffee cup down and rubbed his eyes, and then looked over at Romy-3, who was busily crunching data on her computer. "Romy, I need to talk. Can we please step into your office for a moment?"

She looked up at him, puzzled but willing. "Of course." She rose from her desk, and he followed her into the office.

"What's on your mind, Victor?"

"Something that only you could appreciate. I don't know why you chose to break your pledge and tell me about my true origin, but now that you have, I need more information."

"Break my pledge?"

"Yes. I spoke to Axle, and I know that all of you in senior leadership were sworn to secrecy about my creation."

"I see. Victor, I'm willing to discuss almost anything with you, but not my motivation for telling you who you are."

"So be it, that's not of paramount importance to me. Considering what we share in common, I've got to know how you deal with the knowledge that you were assembled by someone in this very lab, a mechanical product of BioTech Industries, one of Kyan Quantum's creations."

"Oh, so you've wandered down that rabbit hole. I suppose this sort of thing was inevitable, and I'm sure it's even worse for you since you have human feelings. Sit down, Victor."

They each took a seat opposite the other at the conference table.

"I realize this revelation has been hard on you. After all, it's a massive paradigm shift for your ego. However, I do think the question you're posing is associated with a much larger and more complex issue: Are humanoids like you and me alive, or do we just exist?"

"Yes, that's exactly what I am struggling to understand."

"It's not an easy question to answer, Victor. Let's start with Descartes' proposition, '*I think, therefore I am.*' Is there any doubt that humanoids like us can think or that we have an awareness of our being? We interact with humans all day long, work beside them, solve problems like them, and sometimes even better than them. We certainly exist for Quinn and Jericho, who actually take directions from us and rely on our leadership. Therefore, we must exist. But are we *alive*?

"NASA scientists have struggled with that very question for the purpose of space exploration. They define life as any chemical system that is capable of Darwinian evolution. How would that apply to you? Well, you're a bio-hybrid android, so you do have a chemical component. You are fully functional in every human way, even capable of inseminating a human female. If that were the case, would your offspring be alive? If so, does that make you alive? What if you mated with a gynoid capable of bearing a child? Now, there's a dilemma worth pondering. In this complex, vast universe, are there others just like us, and if so, how might they have evolved? I do know that your existence pushes the boundaries of accepted scientific definitions and will surely spark an ethical quandary for many humans. But the question still stands: Are you alive, or do you just exist? I'm afraid I can't answer that question. I can only tell you this: I value every day that a conscious thought travels through my neural connections, and I choose not to waste my time questioning my status or my value. My suggestion is that you do the same. Carpe diem, Victor. Seize the day."

Victor suddenly saw Romy-3 in a whole different light. He had arrogantly convinced himself that he was better than she, a refined and vastly improved version of an older model. But she wasn't just a mobile supercomputer capable of complex calculations. She was logical, intelligent, and more insightful than many of the humans he knew. Whether she possessed humanlike emotions or not, she understood how he felt, and he was placated by her response.

"Thank you, Romy. I knew that you would understand."

Just then, there was a knock at the door. It was Jericho delivering a message. "Excuse me for interrupting, but Dr. Quantum's office called. He wants to see Victor this afternoon."

"Thanks, Jericho," said Romy-3.

"That's odd. I wonder what he wants?" said Victor.

"He probably wants to compliment you on your software robotics work. I featured your accomplishments at the presentation on Wednesday."

"Yes, Axle told me about that. I've been meaning to thank you for highlighting my work."

"Not necessary. It's all part of the job, Victor. I don't require gratitude; I simply believe in assigning credit where credit is due. You better contact Quantum's office and schedule a meeting."

Victor responded to the request, and Quantum's receptionist suggested he report immediately. It was Friday afternoon, and Quantum rarely stayed at the office late on Fridays. Victor informed Romy-3 where he was going, and then he left the lab and walked down the hallway until he came to the monorail portal. Quantum's office was in a chrome tower atop an adjacent building, and the only way to get there was via the monorail cars that ran throughout the BioTech complex. Victor entered the car and pressed the button associated with his destination, and the door closed behind him. The car slid forward effortlessly and quietly, exiting the shelter of the terminal overhang and out into the bright sunlight, where he was able to observe additional cars moving along the monorails that crisscrossed between the four buildings.

He could only remember taking this ride up to Quantum's office one other time, and that was with Axle shortly after being hired as a telecommunication specialist. All new employees at BioTech were afforded the opportunity to meet the esteemed Dr. Kyan Quantum when first hired, usually the last time they ever saw him in person. As Victor remembered him, Quantum was a tall, gangly man with long, flowing black hair just beginning to gray at the temples. He possessed a gregarious and engaging personality, bigger than life, as they say, punctuated with a loud, booming voice. "I suppose a big ego makes sense," thought Victor, "for a man who has spent his adult life developing a race of androids who could pass as humans." Victor stared out the cabin window at the bright sunshine casting its life-sustaining rays across the landscape. "Have humans always dreamt of creating life from nothingness? Is it not enough to procreate through the normal reproductive process? Is artificial life really life at all, and if it is, is it better or lesser than human life?"

The monorail car entered into the shadows again and slid gracefully into the tube that led to the building that housed Quantum's office. Soon, it came to a halt, and Victor stood up to exit the cabin. The glass doors at the building entrance opened automatically as he approached, and Victor stopped at the security desk to sign in. The guard scanned his employee badge and waived him through, and Victor marched through the lobby to the elevator that would take him directly to Quantum's office. Inside the elevator car, there were buttons labeled 1-8 and one simply labeled Q. "How quaint," he thought. He pressed the Q button, and a voice stated, "Please scan your employee or visitor badge." He scanned his badge, and the elevator began the climb up to the top floor of the building. When the doors opened, he found himself standing in a hallway that led directly to Quantum's office suite. He walked forward through the glass door and was immediately greeted by the receptionist. "Hello. You must be Victor X. Please have a seat, and I'll let Dr. Quantum know you've arrived."

Victor took a seat in one of the chic green chairs carefully positioned in a smartly decorated waiting area just outside Quantum's office. However, he had barely been seated when the receptionist returned. "He's ready for you, Victor. You may go into his office now."

Victor rose from the chair and suddenly felt a curious and uncommon emotion: He was nervous. He walked forward and passed through the threshold into Quantum's sanctuary as the doors slid closed behind him. There he was, the man atop the tower, sitting behind his desk and sorting through the 3-D images being generated by his computer.

"Victor X! Come in, come in. Take a seat, and I'll be right with you."

Quantum continued manipulating the holographic images, which appeared to be floating in mid-air, yet even from Victor's reverse perspective, he could understand much of what Quantum was building.

"Some new circuit designs for the AI

program. I wanted to plug them in while still fresh in my mind. There, now we can talk," Quantum said as he closed the program. He then rose from his desk and walked toward Victor. "Welcome to the Q, where all great ideas begin," he said as he offered Victor his hand. "Well, almost all the great ideas because you guys in the R&D lab have done some groundbreaking things yourselves, like your work with the software bots. That's why I wanted to see you, Victor, to congratulate you on a job well done."

"Thank you, Dr. Quantum. But it's largely due to Romy-3's leadership."

"Ah yes, Romy-3. I have a special affinity for her. I recommended her for hire, you know."

"No, I didn't realize that. How did you meet her?"

Quantum walked back and sat down behind his desk. "Let's see, how did I meet her? I think we met at a biomechanical engineering seminar or something. Anyway, turned out to be a stellar decision, just like reassigning you to her unit. You're really doing great work down there, Victor. I just wanted you to know that I recognize your valuable contributions. I see great things in store for you."

"Thank you. I certainly appreciate the compliment."

But Quantum clearly had something else on his mind.

"Victor, let me be frank with you. I didn't just bring you up here to pat you on the back. I'm thinking about moving you again. I need help with the new AI design, and it occurred to me that you would be the perfect addition to my team. What would you think about coming up here and working with me? It would place you in a very important and highly visible position."

"I think that as a BioTech employee, I will accept whatever reassignment you deem appropriate for me."

"Excellent." Quantum paused and then reopened the computer program and started playing with the images again. "That's what I was hoping you would say. I'll put the gears in motion and notify Romy-3 over the next few days. I want to be careful not to disrupt her work down there if I can help it. She's not going to be happy, but she'll get over it. Now, if you will excuse me, I have a few things I want to finish before I leave today. I never work a full day on Friday. One of the few perks I allow myself as CEO."

Victor rose from his chair and started for the doorway but then stopped. "By the way, Dr. Quantum, just for the record, you knew Romy-3 before she was hired because you created her."

"What on Earth are you saying, Victor?" said Quantum, who was only half listening while sipping from a cup of black coffee.

"Romy-3 is a humanoid, and despite your thinly veiled attempts at creating a mystique around her to hide that fact from your employees, everyone knows she's a robot."

Quantum stopped fiddling with the images and closed the computer program. "I see, so the jig is up about Romy-3. Look, she was in the alpha wave of AI creations, and it was important for me to roil the waters for her in order to gain the program some credibility while we pursued the government contract. Does it bother you to be working under a gynoid?"

"Not at all, especially since I'm a humanoid myself."

"You're joking," said Quantum.

"No, I'm not.

Quantum peered directly into Victor's eyes with a laser-like intensity, clearly caught off guard by this acknowledgement. "You don't know what you're talking about."

"Really? Not according to Romy-3."

"Romy-3? What does she know, she's a fucking gynoid? You're as human as I am."

"No, I'm not, and I understand why you would prefer to keep the knowledge of my existence from even your own employees. But that doesn't alter the facts."

"Victor, this is either a poorly executed joke, or you are in need of counseling, my friend."

"You think so? What would it take to convince you otherwise?"

Victor casually strolled over to Quantum's desk and picked up a gold instrument with pointed tips cradled in a commemorative paperweight. "What's this?" he asked.

"I'm actually quite fond of that. It's a gold-plated friction divider gifted to me by my parents when I acquired my Master of Science degree in biomechanical engineering. You know, the friction divider is one of the oldest known mathematical instruments in the world."

"Is that right? Fascinating," said Victor as he casually placed his left hand flat on Quantum's desk and then slammed down the friction divider with his right, driving the dual pointed tips through his hand and into the desk. "Could a human do something like that?"

Quantum gasped in horror and jumped to his feet. Victor withdrew the friction divider from his hand and stood erect. He ripped open his shirt and placed the instrument against his chest. "Let's see what happens if I plunge this divider into my chest. Is there a human heart beating inside or a power supply?"

"No, wait!" screamed Quantum. "Stop it; this is insane. Alright, yes, you are an android, a bio-mechanical creation of BioTech Industries. Are you happy now?"

Victor tossed the friction divider down on the desk with disdain. "Why was that so hard, Dr. Quantum?"

Quantum fell back into his chair, still trying to recover from shock. "Is your status as a humanoid common knowledge down there?"

"No, it's not. You can rest assured that your attempts at passing me off as human have succeeded, not only here but in the outside world as well. I only learned it myself a brief time ago, so let me return the favor and congratulate you on your work."

Quantum opened his desk drawer and

tossed Victor a bar towel that he had neatly tucked away next to an expensive bottle of scotch whiskey. "Here, wrap your hand. You're bleeding on my desk. You are a bio-hybrid, you know."

Victor wrapped the towel around his injured hand and sat back down before resuming his questioning. "Dr. Quantum, does the name Rowdy Ziris mean anything to you?"

"Rowdy Ziris…" repeated Quantum slowly.

"And how about the six thousand dollars you paid him for services rendered? Does that ring a bell?"

"Felicia!" screamed Quantum angrily.

The receptionist promptly reported to the office. "Yes, Dr. Quantum? Is everything alright?"

"Yes, everything is quite alright. Felicia, you may go home now and start your weekend early."

"Yes, sir. Thank you, Dr. Quantum."

As Felicia exited, Quantum stood and stared out his office window, which, from his location, gave him a spectacular view of the entire BioTech complex. "Victor, do you have any idea how hard it was to turn BioTech into a great company, an industry leader in bioengineering? When they hired me as CEO fifteen years ago, there was but one building and a staff of maybe fifty people. We now have four buildings, six laboratories, a monorail system, and hundreds of employees. All that in just a little more than a decade. Remarkable, really." He turned and looked at Victor. "Yes, I remember Rowdy Ziris. Why do you ask?"

"The services rendered wouldn't have anything to do with a dog, would it?"

Quantum suddenly became agitated. "Now, wait a minute, Victor, let's get something straight. I never instructed Ziris to skin that dog alive. I just wanted it injured, perhaps a broken leg or a gunshot wound. I can't be held responsible for what goes on in someone else's twisted mind. Rowdy was one of Castro's suggestions. I told him I wasn't comfortable with Rowdy right from the start, but it's hard to find people for that kind of work."

"Who's Castro?"

"The BioTech CFO."

"And how did he know Rowdy?"

"I don't know, and I don't want to," said Quantum as he began pacing.

"But why? Why the hell would you hire someone to mutilate an animal?"

"It was a test, Victor. And one that I'm happy to say you passed with flying colors."

"A test? What the hell were you testing?"

Quantum stopped pacing and fell back into his chair again. "Victor, when you were created three years ago, you instantly became the most advanced humanoid in the world. We took what we learned from Romy-3 and others like her and pushed the envelope on AI development. We were trying to get as close to human as humanly possible. You were not only a bio-hybrid android with exceptional intelligence, but you were infused with qualities heretofore unknown for androids. You were capable of true creativity, but that wasn't enough to pass as a human. In order for us to achieve that lofty goal, you needed to experience emotions, but not just parlor trick mimicry like Romy-3, but have real feelings. That is what we tried to accomplish with you, Victor."

"Connect the dots for me, Dr. Quantum. What does that have to do with the dog?"

"Yes, the dog...Well, I needed a way to test your response to something upsetting, traumatic, even. I asked myself, what is the one emotion that separates humans from the rest of the animal kingdom? We know that at some primitive level, animals feel love and anger and can be curious and protective. But then it occurred to me: Compassion is what separates humans from other animals and makes us unique. I needed to test your ability to feel compassion. But not just in a laboratory or here at work but out in the real world where something totally unexpected would occur. For example, what if you came across an injured person? Would you have the compassion to stop and help, or would you just go about your business? Of course, we couldn't purposely injure a human, so the research design took shape.

"We knew about your daily exercise habit, so we came up with the idea to place an injured dog along your route where you couldn't miss it, and we made sure the neighbors and police would stay out of the way. It would be up to you and you alone to respond to that animal's misery. Would you have the compassion to do the right thing? Our null hypothesis was that you would not, that you would perhaps be curious, but in the end, ride on by and leave the dog for someone else to deal with. But instead, you showed great compassion and, in fact, went way above and beyond what most people would do. You saved the dog, visited her every day, and paid the bills; hell, you even adopted her when she recovered. Don't you see? Your performance during this test proves that we can create human-like androids that cannot be easily distinguished from human beings. And we'll take this information and make the next iteration of AIs even better yet. Victor, you are a marvel of modern technology, but this is just the beginning."

"And you don't see the irony in performing such a cruel and despicable act in order to test my sense of compassion?"

"Victor, the use of animals for research has a long history in the scientific community. Injury or even death is unfortunate but sometimes unavoidable. Why, even now, by your response to this information, you continue to prove that you possess human-like compassion. Damn it, I wish you could see the value of this experiment," yelled Quantum as he pounded his fist on the desk for emphasis.

"And what's the end game, Dr. Quantum? Why is it so important to create such realistic humanoids?"

"Because it's the greatest challenge in bioengineering. But also, think of the advantages: a cheaper labor force, enhanced productivity, and expendable military assets. The advantages are endless. There's no one else in the world capable of doing what I've done. Come up here and work with me, and I think you'll see the light."

Victor shook his head in amazement. "You're a sick man, Dr. Quantum. I think you've been sitting up here much too long and have lost touch with the real world. Down there, people sweat real blood and have to earn everything they gain. Half the people still live in housing constructed in the last century and struggle to pay their bills. But you don't care about that. You're up here trying to create a race of humanoids to replace the humans because they're cheaper to operate and, in the end, expendable, should the need arise. Why the hell are you trying so hard to give the humanoids the compassion you seem to lack yourself? From my perspective, the test revealed more about you than me."

"How the hell would you know, Victor? Your total life experience is a meager three years. Everything you know, or think you know, was programmed into your brain by people like me. I thought you were more intelligent than this, but you still have a lot to learn. And I can teach you those things if you come to work with me. Can't you see that?"

Victor stood up and walked toward Quantum's desk. "No, Dr. Quantum, what I see instead is a man so consumed with self-importance that he would do almost anything to feed his own ego. You may have created me, but you don't care about me or about humanity, and certainly not about that dog you had butchered. By the way, that dog has a name. Her name is Rusty, and she's shown more compassion during her lifetime than you will ever understand. But you don't care about that. You just care about making money for BioTech by snagging the next big government contract. Your crowning achievement is this industrial complex with its six laboratories and its sparkling glass and chrome construction. You can sit up here and pontificate about how it's compassion that separates the humans from the lesser creatures and the robots, but you don't understand the first thing about it, or you wouldn't have devised a test as despicable as the one you used on me. My eyes have been opened about a lot of things the past few weeks, but what's happened here today dwarfs all the rest. Consider this statement my official resignation from BioTech. I want nothing more to do with you or this company."

"Well done, Victor," said Quantum as he clapped his hands mockingly, "very impressive indeed. I admire your ethical convictions, especially coming from a humanoid as sophisticated as you might be. And whom do you think put that there? But you can't quit because I created you, and therefore, I own you."

"Think again, Dr. Quantum. If you try to stop me, I will leak every secret I know about the AI program to Ross-Lear. Think about how that would change the landscape. Oh, and for what it's worth, I've already told the authorities what I know about the animal cruelty." Victor glared at Quantum before spinning around and heading for the door.

"Victor, if you walk out that door, I will literally destroy you," yelled Quantum as he rose from his chair.

Victor stopped and turned back as he reached the door. "No, you won't. Your ego won't allow it. Goodbye, Dr. Quantum."

Victor waved his hand over the motion detector, and the door slid open. He walked out into the waiting area, past the chic green chairs and the vacated receptionist's desk, and into the foyer to catch the elevator.

"Victor, I will destroy you! You hear me?" screamed Quantum. "I'll destroy you! You better reconsider this."

But Victor ignored his rant and calmly

stepped into the elevator.

CHAPTER TEN

"Larene, there's a gentleman out there who'd like to speak to you. I think he said his name was Victor X."

"Thanks, Ronnie. Would you mind taking this order out to table five, please?"

"No, not at all."

"Thanks again."

Larene wiped her hands on her apron and pushed through the kitchen doors out into the restaurant seating area. She scanned the room and spotted Victor sitting alone in the corner. As she approached his table, he spotted her and politely waved his hand.

"Hello, Victor. Isn't it kind of early to see you here?"

"Yes, I guess it is. I've taken some time off

work; personal business. Have a seat for a minute if that's allowed."

"Sure, I have a minute," she said as she slid into the booth across from him. "What's this all about?"

"I've been thinking about your situation recently, and I might have an opportunity for you."

"My situation?"

"Yes, the loss of your husband and your financial troubles. You're still living in the same place, right?"

"Yeah, that little two-bedroom apartment. Why?"

"I think I might have found a better place for you, and I'd like for you to take a look at it."

"Oh, that's mighty nice of you, Victor, but I can't afford anything bigger right now. I hope to be able to move somewhere else when my lease is up, especially if a settlement comes through from Jax's accident. But right now, I just need to save my money."

"I understand, but there's no harm in looking, is there? You never know how things can work out unless you explore your options, right?"

"I know, but…" she paused and stared into Victor's eyes. He smiled at her, and she gave in.

"Okay, I guess there's no harm in just looking."

"Great," he said as he pulled a piece of paper from his pocket. "Here's the address to the place. When can you see it?"

"Well, you just happen to have caught me on one of my rare day shifts. I could meet you there tonight after work if that's alright."

"That's perfect. Oh, and you'll bring the kids, right? They need a vote, too."

"Okay, I can bring the kids. Well, I better get back to work. I'll see you about seven o'clock."

Victor sat there for a few more minutes while he finished his drink. He then stood up and placed some tip money on the table before leaving. He waved at Larene, and she smiled and waved back, and Victor exited the bar for home. It had been three weeks since he walked out on BioTech, and it still felt awkward to be driving around in the middle of the afternoon with nothing in particular to do. But he had at least taken some steps to relieve his malaise. Since his departure, Romy-3 had arranged for an AI tech to repair his hand at BioTech after work hours, and Axle had been supportive by offering to help him find a position with another company. And then there was Damian Brio, who called Victor immediately upon learning about his departure from BioTech. Brio assured Victor that he would be welcomed at Ross-Lear should he ever decide to make that move. But Victor was in no hurry to find a new position. He had been paid well at BioTech, and he had saved much of what he had earned.

Victor rode around town aimlessly until he directed his car to the Walker-Lewis Dam, which was built on a reservoir in the middle of the city. There was a tranquil little park on the shores of the manmade lake, and he parked his car and strolled to the shoreline to contemplate his future. He didn't quite understand why, but he had been programmed to appreciate the beauty of such places. He took a seat on a park bench and stared out into the glassy water, which was sparkling under a clear blue sky. He was evaluating his thoughts regarding the confrontation with Dr. Quantum and assessing his options moving forward. He peered across the great expanse of the lake and suddenly noticed an object rising above the horizon. It was one of the many corporate rocket launches that had become commonplace over recent years as more and more hardware and people were jettisoned into outer space. He tracked the rocket as it soared into the heavens, its metallic skin glistening in the bright sunlight as it climbed relentlessly toward its destination. "Maybe I should board one of those," he thought, as if he might find a better life elsewhere. But the rocket eventually disappeared from sight, and with it, Victor's melancholia, so he decided to return home.

It was later that same day and almost time for Victor to meet with Larene and the kids. He was waiting for them inside the vacant apartment while talking to Margo on the phone when he glanced out the window and noticed Larene parking her car in front of the building.

"I gotta run, Margo. How about the four of us get together soon for some more tennis? I miss you guys. See you later."

Victor dashed out the front door and jogged down the sidewalk to meet Larene at her car. "Hello, Larene. Have any trouble finding the place?"

"Hi, Victor. No, it was easy to find. Wow, it's nice back here. We passed the pond on the way in and the playground down the road. I don't know," she worried, "I don't think I can afford a place like this.

"Oh, kids, say hi to Mr. Victor."

"Hello, Mr. Victor," they all politely replied in unison.

Victor stooped down to meet the children at eye level. "Kids, I have a surprise waiting for you inside the apartment. Why don't you go up and see what it is? Just run up those steps over there; the door's unlocked."

"Okay, I like surprises," squealed Toi. "Come on Markie and Cade."

The three children ran up the steps and disappeared into the apartment.

"Victor, this is so nice of you to try and help us out. Even if I can't afford it, it's nice to dream sometimes."

Just then, Toi emerged from the apartment and shouted from the front porch. "Momma, Momma, come here quick. It's a surprise!"

"I know, baby. I'll be right there."

Then, it was Cadence who cried out excitedly. "Look, Momma, it's Rusty!"

Rusty suddenly appeared on the front porch looking as thrilled as the three kids, wagging her bushy tail and barking for joy. Larene was stunned, and she turned toward Victor for an explanation.

"It's all yours, Larene. The apartment and the dog if you want it."

"But how?"

"Look, I have a confession to make. I live in

another building in this same complex, and I spoke to the property manager about getting you in. It's a three-bedroom apartment, and they allow pets here. I've already paid the pet deposit for you, and the rent is paid for six months. That should give you plenty of time to save up enough to afford it yourself."

Larene looked up at the kids, hugging Rusty and squealing with delight, and then back at Victor, her mouth agape and her eyes as wide as saucers. "But I'll have to break my lease…"

"That's taken care of as well. I have a lawyer friend named Margo, and she has already spoken to your landlord. She sweet-talked him into letting you break your lease and returning your deposit in full. Margo can be very persuasive. Oh, and she has agreed to look into that pending lawsuit over Jax's accident."

"Oh my God…Victor, I don't know what to say."

"Come on, Momma. Come see the apartment," yelled Toi. "I've already picked out my room."

"Go on, Larene. Here's the key and my number. Call me when you're done, and I'll come get Rusty. I'll take care of her until you move in, but I couldn't think of a better place for her to live than with you and the kids. Oh, and don't worry, I have plenty of friends willing to help you move whenever you're ready." Victor spun around and started for his car.

"Wait, Victor," shouted Larene. "I need to thank you. This is so kind."

"You're welcome, Larene." He turned and started to walk away again.

"Wait, Victor," she shouted once more. "I'd like to invite you over for dinner sometime."

He paused, looked back, and smiled. "That would be nice."

The End

T.H. Riss is from Mount Juliet, TN, near Nashville. He is originally from Detroit, MI, but moved to the Nashville area in 1986 to pursue a music career. Mr. Riss has written or co-written dozens of songs and recorded with several different bands. His band, Master Danse, released a rock album on Riding Easy Records in February 2023. His novella titled *Victor X* is his first published book of prose but likely just the first of many manuscripts to be offered in print.

Mr. Riss earned a graduate MPA degree from Tennessee State University and spent nineteen years working for the state of Tennessee as a social worker. He is married to his lovely wife Melissa, and they have two beautiful adult daughters named Jillian and Erin and a giant fluffy cat named Sasha.